EDDIE & EMILY

EDDIE & EMILY

AND THE DEMON CELL

B. R. LEWIS

EDDIE & EMILY
AND THE DEMON CELL

B.R. LEWIS

Print edition ISBN: 9780473650322
E-book edition ISBN: 9780473650346
Hardback edition ISBN: 9780473651787
Dust Jacketed edition ISBN: 9780473651794

First edition: August 2022
10 9 8 7 6 5 4 3 2 1

FOR MY FAMILY,

FROM WHERE THE STRONGEST BONDS

ARE FORMED AND THE MOST

PRECIOUS MEMORIES CHERISHED

INTRODUCTION

Our story begins in the most unlikely of places, at the most unlikely of times in history with probably the most unlikely and surprising characters you could imagine. What's more, this story is quite unlike any traditional fables. Our hero seems to be the most questionable and least motivated of characters and our maiden is equally unexpected, as she seems to be entirely normal for her age. Our hero is a timid, reclusive boy; our maiden is a strong-willed, often flawed schoolgirl. Our hero hides a terrible secret, both powerful and terrifying. Our maiden thinks supernatural powers belong in fairytales and has never known terrible secrets. He is confused about his true purpose. She is eager to learn hers. Still, they are destined to overcome the odds together and in the most startling way imaginable, and, as in most fables, our heroes have no idea of the danger that lies in their immediate future.

What could possibly be worse?

The city is Doon, New Anderson, and our story starts in the wettest, coldest, and most depressing days of Eddie's life as it is winter in August for the people living on the many scattered islands of the southern Oceania archipelago that makes up what used to be the protectorate of the enormous Moray Empire. Eddie and his companions have chosen to arrive on what must be the worst day (in Eddie's opinion) they could have possibly imagined.

Eddie has other reasons to be depressed, that far outweigh his care for the weather. He is of course sad because he had to leave El Anil - the place where Jack, Mom and Eddie had spent the last ten years. He loved LINQ. It was the smells, the tastes, and the warmth but, most of all, it was the escape from the burden of being noticed by anyone. In LINQ, no-one cared or even knew he existed, and Eddie liked it that way. There are that many people in El Anil no-one truly knows how many live there. Eddie was grateful for this because it had been deemed necessary for them to remain utterly unnoticeable, no matter where they went.

That had all changed since Sharma found them hiding in the slums. Sharma was old, very old, and even his youthful bits looked old. He had wrinkles on his wrinkles. His voice was deep and yet sometimes sounded like rustling paper, and his movements could appear slow like a cat who can't decide whether to go out the door or stay inside. But Sharma had authority. Eddie knew (as did Jack and Mom) that when Sharma spoke, you listened, very carefully. Back in El Anil when Sharma had first found Eddie and his companions, it had taken years for Eddie to fully trust him and accept the old man as a teacher (of sorts) yet, over time, Eddie had grown to like him very much. The Sharma had a strange way of communicating that was sometimes regarded as a bit odd and even though Sharma did not seem to ever direct his conversation to or at Eddie, Eddie knew he was directing him, nonetheless. As much as Eddie disliked Sharma's instructions to relocate to New Anderson, he understood enough to know that mistrusting the Sharma would be very unwise. Besides that, Jack, his stepfather in his usual manner, had calmly assured Eddie.

"Trust the old man as I do, Eddie, and one day you will gain the knowledge you so desperately desire!' Jack had implored. If Eddie was unsure about the Sharma's intentions, he certainly wasn't in any way unsure of Jack's. Eddie loved Jack like a father and trusted both 'Mom' (what he affectionately called his 'stepmother') and Jack with his life. He was indebted to them for finding him after he had been abandoned by his genetic birth parents. They protected him as a youngling and eventually taught him some of the unique skills the Sharma had taught them many years before.

This didn't change the fact Eddie was slightly more than disappointed that his life had been turned upside down by Sharma, whom, although Eddie greatly respected, was a bit beyond his 'use by' date. Eddie would now be noticed by hundreds of people who would remember his face every day and he was exhausted by the very thought of people prying into his deeply personal existence. But more than anything, Eddie was angry at the Sharma for insisting that he spend the next 10 years at school learning what Eddie considered worthless dribble.

If anything, Doon's weather quite aptly reflected Eddie's mood that day. The dreary grey sky seemed to close in on him, making him feel even more trapped and claustrophobic, and the cold rain beating hard against the windows of the unnaturally cold tram car was unnerving. "Do these people *not care* that it's freezing in here!" he thought to himself. "They must all be raving mad to not feel the cold." In Eddie's opinion the locals seemed to have a boring, unfriendly, detached way about them. As he travelled on the tram out from the city to the suburb of Carroll Bay, he noticed them hurrying in the downpour going about their discernibly meaningless lives. They seemed to loathe their existence just as much as Eddie did at that moment.

To Eddie, Doon was not just a cold place full of people who hated their lives, it was deeper than that. The drab seemingly colorless identical rows of weatherboard houses all with single chimneys spitting their mutual approbation of disgust merged with Eddie's disapproval. Even more so when he saw the many cathedrals and churches with their dark, grey and ominous demeanors mingling in a collective worship of the dreary. Most of all, it reminded Eddie of Moray. It was as if he could imagine the old Morakin Governors and designers of the city 175 years before, infected by the same colorless neglect and lack of imagination, and all they could create was copies of the same dreary towns they had left behind in Moray. The clever reader of this story might wonder how a 10-year-old boy could ever have witnessed Moray and the places Eddie was pondering over.

Be that as it may, Doon was a beautiful place. Its harbor was perfect for shipping and fishing and the city was flanked by lush tree-lined hills that overlooked the center of the town like sentinels guarding a precious stone. It wasn't a big city at all, not like the bustling, dirty metropolis of El Anil or Torr. As Eddie looked up at the hills lining the harbor, the weather broke for a few minutes and the clouds cleared, revealing the eastern side of the harbor. He noticed a small castle far off atop the tallest hill. Eddie's eyesight must've been extraordinary. A person would have to possess extremely good vision indeed to have a chance of catching a glimpse of the castle and that would be on a clear day too.

The chance sighting of the castle broke him from his sad reverie. If even for a few brief moments, Eddie's dry humor was not wasted on it as he reflected on his distaste for Moray colonization. Eddie found it oddly amusing.

"Boy, they had to bring everything with them, didn't they?" he chuckled to himself. "Castles 'n all!"

"Those Moray's were crazy!" He mused aloud. Amused at the very Morakin insistence on building grand architecture to further impose their supremacy over everyone wherever they went. Despite Eddie's bias and brutal judgement of the early Moray settlers, the castle was magnificent. As he viewed it from a distance, he wondered if he would be able to see the entire city from its elevated ramparts. His inquisitive nature dislodged his dejected state momentarily and he broke free to wonder at the mental state of its original owner. "A man who has to look down on his investments every day, is a man who has great need of a break." Eddie quoted some obscure book's contents thoughtfully.

A few minutes later and to Eddie's surprise the tramcar was nearing their stop. That Doon was small by Linq city standards was a welcome reprieve for anyone.

“We’re almost there,” Jack announced to no-one and everyone, who had been silent for their entire journey from the Airship Terminal to the town which, because of Doons spectacular hills, was quite a distance from the city.

“Oh goodie!” Eddie replied sarcastically, “I was going to burst with excitement....” He couldn’t finish. Jack didn’t really seem like he was in a joking mood today and it looked like they were in for a very wet walk from the bus-stop to their new home.

“Excited or not, you can carry some bags!” remarked Mom with schoolteacher-like authority. Both Jack and Eddie regarded Mom with serious looks before she broke the tension with a playful wink at Jack. Gathering her thoughts and taking the chance to assert some authority, she spoke to them quietly like a mother would whisper to her children.

“We are but a few minutes away from safety and refreshment” she said in her strange Isin accent (not unlike an eastern European accent). “Let us be of one mind and focused.”

What Mom said to them had an immediate effect. Eddie tried to focus on finishing their short journey whilst observing the stress that had started to cross Jack’s face. His jaw seemed more clenched than usual as if he held a heightened sense of danger inside.

Perhaps Jack was equally challenged by their new surroundings and needed to break the tension in his own way. He had regrettably suggested that they use ‘normal’ forms of transport, until he could ascertain the risk of discovery. Eddie had reluctantly agreed but, the truth was, he had little choice and Mom was always so amazing at powerfully communicating such intense demands without uttering a word. So, for the time being, he would endure the limitations set on him and try to resign himself to this discouragement he felt and instead focus on what his new mission might entail. If Eddie had any positive change in his mood at all, it was when they finally made it to their new abode. After walking in the sodding wet from the tram stop, down the main road until a winding lane led back up the hill to a dead end, they finally arrived. The houses were not impressive at all. Most of them needed a good paint and the gardens, if you could call them that, were all extremely overgrown. They were either local council or government housing for sure. The whole street in fact. Jack had gotten their dilapidated excuse for a 'home' by writing to the New Anderson Ministry of Immigration and had managed to convince the local bureaucrats to sign off on refugee visas. On one side of the street the houses were much higher up than the others and behind those was a large patch of pine trees that seemed to carry on up to the top of the hill. The small, steep forest gave the impression of hidden secrets and of new places to explore, which held an irresistible appeal to Eddie.

Their 'house' was almost at the end of the cul-de-sac, up high and almost hidden behind the overgrown hedge that grew on the street side. Eddie was, for the first time in a long while, delighted. Any other kid would probably have cried as it wasn't much to look at, however Eddie wasn't like 'other' kids. This would be his refuge. His place.

"Heck, even burglars wouldn't stray down here!" he mused to himself.

Mom moved quickly now as they made their way to the front entrance. She started softly saying a prayer in a language Eddie was well familiar with.

Herra siunaa tätä kotia. siunaa sen matkustajia. siunaa niitä, jotka tulevat, ja niitä, jotka menevät. Tee tämä kotiin ja Bounty turvallisuus. Ehkä se on meidän kartano, kunnes perimme omasi. Antakaa meille voimaa, voimaa ja nöyryyttä, joka tekee sen niin........ she trailed off, seeming impatient to get on with something of significant urgency to her. Jack understood immediately and closed the door behind them, then the curtains, or what was left of them. Neither Jack, Eddie nor Mom ventured any further into the house to look. They did not check to see if there was any power or a fireplace for heat or cooking. They immediately went and stood together in a circle in the middle of the small room at the front. Perhaps you could call it a lounge, but that would be stretching the meaning of the word.

The house was dark, but even in the darkness one could make out several noticeable and awful observations. The house had a terrible odor of moldy curtains and the carpet smelt like a fair amount of foul liquor had been spilt. Not only the missing windowpanes but the cracked and broken ones let in the moisture making it even more unpleasant.

Silently, they stood there as if momentarily becoming mannequins in a secret counsel. One would be forgiven for thinking this behavior a little strange, to not even unpack your bags or go and check out the beds or the fridge, does seem bizarre. Mom started murmuring something that sounded like ancient Hebrew or Arabic. If you had been there, you would have sworn that it sounded like a church hymn, only in an indecipherable language. You would probably have thoroughly enjoyed the sound too; had you not been utterly distracted by what was happening inside the room.

Everything was changing in the room. The smelly threadbare carpet had become a beautiful deep red color and the drapes dark velvet purple. Even the size of the room seemed to have changed. It had become bigger, and a huge fireplace had appeared, sat in the center of the newly now massive room. Elegant furnishings appeared. Tables, chairs, bookcases full of old literature, desks and ornate moldings were created on the now much higher ceilings with grand lighting and chandeliers. What was before, the tiny front door, was now an entrance. An appealing tiled entrance was now their atrium. The front door was of course unrecognizable, for now the entry was a solid wooden door with a large brass lion on the inside of the door. Peculiar to have what looks akin to a knocker on the inside of the door? Before, the house had had an awful stale smell of liquor, cigarette butts and moldy walls, but now the smell of sweet incense wafted throughout the house. Everywhere a new invigorating scent pervaded.

Had you chosen to look further and venture up the stairs, you would have noticed that this magic had transformed every single room of the house and each floor seemed to have a different style or era associated with it. What is more astonishing, is that there seemed to be more levels than there had been before. The top level, (was it 3 or 4?), It had an almost Mediterranean feel. It even felt like it was warm comparable to the Adriatic in summer.

Eddie, Jack, or Mom didn't stop improving until the house was complete, and they were satisfied with their new home. Mom disappeared to the kitchen and came back a few minutes later with a tray of exquisite food for Jack and Eddie. They ate in silence, then whispered their mutual approval to each other. They were exhausted but had one more task to finish. They stepped outside into the cold, now dark, evening.

The house was still, as it had been before. No sign of the magnificent home that lay within.

"Eet isss dunn." She hummed to herself in quiet satisfaction. "Job well done, Mom" Jack said in a hushed tone. Eddie nods his silent blessing and they quietly retreated into their mysteriously disguised haven. Across the street a child was going to bed. A young girl happened to notice three figures step out of their house into the rain for a moment and huddle there. She couldn't see what for as it was quite dark, and they were hard to make out, but she did think it was a bit peculiar. Exciting though, she thought to herself. Tomorrow she would tell her mum about the new neighbors. "I'll bet my mum hasn't got a clue 'bout them at all!" she wondered excitedly before closing her curtains.

Earlier that day, in a school just up the hill there was a girl named Emily.

Emily was having a terrible day. It was only morning break, and she was currently hiding in the library closet, in what was probably the most neglected school, in her opinion, in the history of educational institutions. She had been outraged that Miss Beadle, her Year 6 teacher, most likely in her 90's, had sent her to the principal's office for apparently provoking Brent Smith, whom she disliked immensely, into a fight. Miss Beadle clearly did not want to get Brent into trouble even though he had started the disagreement. This infuriated Emily as she knew Beadle was a massive suck-up to Brent's dad. Mr. Smith, Brent's father had inherited a small fortune from his grandmother on his mother's side when she passed away a few years earlier. Since he did not care for investing his money in stock markets, he had instead bought a fishing boat and hired a couple of deckhands for a few seasons. His choice had been a good one and it suited his rough nature as people like Brent's dad didn't mingle well in society as they tended to upset them far too regularly often. This is perhaps where Brent learnt his obnoxious behavior, but rumor had it that his mum possessed an equally fantastic library of choice words to use when properly goaded.

Miss Beadle was such an enormous suck up to Brent's dad, not just because she feared both him and his wife but mostly because her grandson was working on one of Mr. Smith's boats and she didn't want him losing his job because if Brent 'narked' on her to his dad. Emily thought the old lady was the most despicable soft touch she had ever met.

So, the outspoken Emily had taken the rap for Brent's fondness to use his fists to settle disputes. Miss Beadle might have been old and morally questionable, but she was also cunning. Her appearance was a sort of explosion of grey and brown made more unbearable by the odor of tea, cigarettes, and perm (a kind of hair setting potion used in hair salons). Because of her oversized hair curlers, her head kind of bobbed when she got agitated and her head would give the impression that it was bouncing. Miss Beadle undoubtably disliked Emily, mostly because she spoke her mind and girls were not supposed to speak up or even dare to question adults. It wasn't going to end well. Emily would often have to hold back her laughter when she saw Miss Beadle becoming flustered, which didn't need much encouragement.

But not today. Today was different. Her world had changed. It had become a hard, callous place that was indifferent to her dilemma. Today there was no amusement in her clever mockery of her teacher.

Today she had used her self-righteous offense at Brent as a cover for her own fragility and she had come apart. Emily had been hiding in the cramped closet because of how she truly felt. Usually, she would have enjoyed the conflict with Brent and Miss Beadle, but not today. Emily was crying. In truth, she was sobbing. She was hiding because she didn't want anyone knowing how sad she really was. The unvarnished truth would have been far too much for Emily to divulge to anyone. The night before, her father, Wayne, had left without saying goodbye. That was not unusual of course, except that this time Emily felt like she would never see him again. Wayne had often been away from home and seemed to be spending more time away because of his work or whatever it was that he did when he left for weeks. Emily had begun to feel that she was a nuisance to him, and his manner seemed to suggest that his mind was always elsewhere.

Despite that, Emily had cherished the time she did spend with him, and she missed their chats about world events on the news. Her Dad meant everything to her, and it was as though he was her own superhuman hero at times. Emily had regarded her parents as unbreakable as granite but her shelter in her innocence was beginning to come apart. Emily really did miss her dad and felt she would not ever stop believing that he loved her even if had left them. Besides, her memories were her treasure! They had sat through the Oceania Games broadcast and had even watched the opening on the TV! and in color! She had been flabbergasted when her dad had brought home the new TV set as a special treat for them. Times were good once.

The night before, Emily had pretended to be asleep while her parents argued loudly in the kitchen. There was a lot of shouting and accusations, 'You said you were going to be there!' and 'I don't have to tell you anything!' There was lots of shouting, but after a while Emily had closed her mind off to it and fallen asleep. In the morning her Mum, Pamela, was sitting at the kitchen table with her head in her hands, looking weary and red eyed from what was obviously no sleep and many tears. Emily had said nothing, not a word. She had quietly gotten herself ready and left for school, giving her Mum what she hoped was a soft reassuring squeeze on the hand before leaving. Emily could not say anything that morning. Not because she did not want to, but because she did not want to bawl in front of her Mum, and she thought she had much more self-control.

She was wrong.

Emily was determined not to let Miss Beadle and that awful boy Brent get the better of her however, so she made her way eventually to the principal's office. She was neither afraid or worried, in fact the office was a safe place for her and the principal, even though a tall middle-aged serious man, was quite kind to Emily and had always been immensely helpful to her. Emily knocked apprehensively at his office door.

A gruff reply was heard, and the shuffling of feet could be heard as the principal Dr David Moot made his way to the door to open it for Emily.

"Oh, Emily. He stared down his nose through his reading glasses blearily. "Trouble with that Smith boy again, yes?" The principal was well ahead of the game and for a grumpy looking old teacher he had an almost magical ability to discern the many social disturbances that lay within his classrooms. Emily blushed but the principal regarded her kindly and offered her his seat. "You shall have the punishment of having to chat with me for a while then, eh? Dr Moot winked at her his best. She returned his jest with a disproving look of mock judgment.

"Come, He said, now seeing she had relaxed a bit. "Let's chat for a while and then you can go back to your class in a bit, yes?". They did and the chat was good for Emily and even perhaps a welcome diversion for Dr Moot too. By the time she had left the principal's office her mood had changed from one of dejected self-pity to one off confidant self-assurance.

So, as she re-entered her classroom in an air of casual defiance that could be perceived as arrogance, Emily masters her emotions and tries to cover a smile.

Some of the kids regarded her with quiet "ooohs" and "hmmmphs." One even manages a quiet snicker. Had you been there, you could not be capable or ignoring the fact that Emily is equally admired by some of her classmates as she is also disliked.

You see, Emily was not a 'know-it-all' kid who gloated to the others. No, not at all. Emily was humble. Her only fault, in Miss Beadle's judgment, was that she asked questions. She would strike you as being the only one not afraid to speak up and as history has revealed to us, the Emily's of this world are often loved and hated coequally among the population.

Emily's satisfaction at this reprieve was short lived and she is soon lost in the sea of her unresolved feelings again. As much as her mixed emotions threatened to knock her off her perch of self-control and no matter how much she dreads seeing her mum after school, Emily resolves to persevere.

She remembered that she has her music lesson after school. What a fortunate distraction from irritating, nosy kids that only drew immense amusement from her discomfort. Emily did love playing the Piano. She was fortunate that her family owned a piano. It was a gift from her grandmother who had died only last year. It had dark wood and humble yet elegant candle holders at the front. She would enjoy lighting the candles and practicing her pieces given to her by her tutor. The sound and feel of the piano were to her, a balm for her senses and an escape from the worries of her distress.

Her Piano lesson was a dream and her teacher, even though an elderly woman living alone, was quite a bit like Emily. Quick to speak her mind, not afraid to issue criticism, but always encouraging and cheerful. Emily and her tutor were like two kindred spirits and together they enjoyed Emily's lessons very much. Her mood couldn't possibly have deflated now. She was on a high, riding a wave of personal satisfaction at achieving her musical goal of playing her newest piece to the end without a single mistake.

Pam, her Mum, was waiting to pick her up when she finished. Emily's mood was instantly deflated. As she walked towards the car, she noticed her Mum swallow her own, clearly troubled, emotions. It was especially obvious to Emily when her Mum didn't speak. Pam just started the car and began the short drive home. Emily was thankful the journey was a short one as the tension in the car was more than a bit awkward, nonetheless, before they made it into the house, her mum stopped and faced her in the driveway.

"I'm sorry, Bun," (Mum always called her that) said Pamela, trying to find the words.

"I, I, ... Don't think he is coming back this time." Pam was in tears again.

"It's okay Mum" pressed Emily, thinking that she had to be the strong one.

Pam hugged her. "No, it's not OK Bun, but we will survive." Pam managed a brief smile.

Her hug had a dual effect on Emily and Pamela. They both had expressed a mutual consideration for each other's feelings and Emily's need to suppress her tears was dissolved by her mother's attention to her. Her tears were now a mixture of relief, sadness, and the joy of being needed and loved. Pamela needed to be needed right now and Emily's extraordinary discernment of her feelings was translated in her simple hug.

For now, things were okay.

That night, wearied from the days up and downs, Emily slept remarkably well. It was not her sleep that was particularly odd however, it was the dream she had that was exceptionally bizarre.

Dreams are for most people, bizarre. You probably couldn't recall a single dream in which you contemplated its content to be normal. There is always one or two surreal objects or events that appear in your dream that let you know you are in fact just dreaming. Many have woken from these terrifying examples of their own imagination and caught themselves before upending into madness and exclaiming to the darkness, "Oh, that was just a dream. Go back to sleep silly!"

Emily's dream was, from her perspective just that: a confusing collection of great and powerful events. In her young innocent mind, even as discerning as she was for her age, the dream was far too terrible to be true and had she ever chanced to see a half decent sci-fi movie that is what she would have described it to you as.

For in her dream, she stood on a far hilltop overlooking a huge city. A metropolis with the tallest buildings she could imagine, and it sprawled its tendrils as far as her eye could see. These towering structures, we call them skyscrapers now, could have numbered in the thousands, she could not tell. As in all dreams, some events appeared to happen in slow motion.

A multitude of huge flying machines, warships appeared in the sky above the city, and she saw the attack.

She witnessed the explosions and the breathtaking contempt for innocent lives orchestrated by the brutal attackers. She wept. In her dream she was sobbing and crying out for those who were dying. She could hear the screams of the victims and each blast of every bomb. She could not do anything. Paralyzed and unable to move from the spot where she stood rooted, she watched in horror as the attack moved slowly towards her. The frustration of being powerless to defend those people or to even shout to the attackers was unbearable to her. She was Emily, a person wholly unafraid to speak up but now she was locked in her passive witness to its terror. Its stupendous size and breadth of the attacking force was so overwhelming that she feared she might stop breathing.

And suddenly, Emily felt like she was being watched, like eyes far off could see her and were gloating at her terror. Emily had the feeling that such evil was amused by her compassion for the victims. A lone gunship arose directly in front of her. Still unable to move, Emily struggled to call out in her dream for help. She mouthed the words, but nothing came out. Her devastation was almost upon her and there seemed nothing she could do to stop it.

The Gunship burst into flame. A loud explosion rocked the hillside as the gunship scattered its shattered torso across the hill. Had she been saved? Had the others? Who had saved them? Why couldn't she call for help?

And there, as if by magic, a man stood in front of her. The scene around them had cleared. He was a darker skinned, handsome man in his mid-twenties. He was addressing her directly.

He knew her. Who was he? Was he going to kill me?

Then she heard him. He spoke slowly and softly amid the chaos. "Emily, it's time to go." And she woke up.

CHAPTER 01
NEW HOMES

The day before, George, an elderly reclusive man, set out with his three dogs to walk along the peninsula. George may have been old, but he could walk for hours. Content in his solitude. That morning, he had set off from Carroll Bay on the peninsula bus with his dogs. You see, the bus took him right out to the last little village (Portobello) on the harbour side of the cape. Roughly eight miles one way was far too much for George to walk even if he did enjoy a good stroll. Normally any bus driver in their right mind would have told George to sod off with his dogs yet the driver always disregarded this rule. All the drivers knew George and his dogs and were used to dropping him at the head of the peninsula. A boon that George would often gruffly welcome.

"Aye up," he would utter to the driver in an accent that might have compared quite easily to Welsh. Only on a good day though, normally all the drivers would get was a severe nod in their direction.

The driver was neither offended nor remotely interested in George's lack of manners, but he would occasionally voice his concern in George's direction.

"Mind those bloody dogs of yours's old man! I don't want no letters to the station master, right!" the driver warned George but only half-heartedly. He knew there were always people who sat behind desks, their life's purpose caught up in finding out what next thing needed to be complained about, and then writing dozens of 'letters-to-the-editor' like a broken record, until hopefully someone came along and threw the player out the window.

The place where George walked that day was far out near the opening of the harbour where the sides were at their most narrow. You could most probably shout to someone on the other side on a fair day with a gentle breeze. There, the vista closely resembled the Scottish coasts in the north. The cold sea air and the gentle sloping green hills scattered with tussock and the occasional sheep would fill any Scot with a surge of nostalgia. If George had ever seen Scotland, he might've cared but I very much doubt it.

George hadn't always been a recluse. Many years earlier, he had a wife and a son, but his wife had left him when his son was just a baby, supposedly never to be seen again. George had tried to find them but hadn't succeeded. As fate would have it, the son had pleaded with his mother later in life to tell him his father's identity. Back then, you could not get a DNA test and if someone was clever enough to change your birth records you would never learn who your 'real' dad was, but she had taken her secret to her grave and denied both George and his son the restitution they both longed for. George had returned to Doon later in life, having given up on his search many years earlier. Little did he know that his son was living only a few streets away. The son would occasionally see the old man walking up the hill with his dogs even on the coldest, wettest days. He would often walk to the corner store on his way home from after work and curse the old man for enjoying the wretched weather so much. The son now had his own offspring that George of course, would also never meet.

That son's name was Brent.

George, however, was oblivious to all this dramatic irony and was in his element, walking in the quiet solitude with only the sound of the waves, the birds and the occasional enthusiastic bark of his dogs running after a hare. There was not a soul in sight, indeed, even the royal bird watching nutters weren't out on the heads today, or so he thought. In 1982 the peninsula wasn't what it is today. Today it's busy with tourist buses going out to see the penguin and albatross colonies and dotted along the harbour is a growing spectacle of boutique accommodation. George probably would have hated it.

All reclusive men shun the fellowship of his peers, or anyone in George's case, and it can be both an advantage and a disadvantage. On this day it would prove to be a supreme disadvantage, for George was very soon going to die. All men die, that much is plain. Yet George does not die a horrific gruesome violent death involving a powerful struggle. No, not at all. If there's anything sad about George's death it is because of his unresolved misfortune in life, not his character. George's life would just – end, or would it?

George ventured with his three dogs past the old, abandoned gun emplacements and military tunnels, left there after a long-forgotten war many decades earlier. One of his dogs chased after a hare down into the long tunnel leading into the hill.

"Stupid mutt" he snarled. "That bleedin' dog!" he cursed to himself. George called after it and whistled to the dog but to no avail. He would have to go and get him. "Darn bleedin' mutt!" he exclaimed, his short temper almost about to burst forth.

And so, he went after his dog, down into the darkened tunnel, whilst yelling at his other dogs to stay back and made his way down into the blackness. He didn't make it very far though and he needn't have worried for his dogs. In fact, George would never worry again.

For George was dead. His heart had literally just stopped, and I doubt even if he'd been right outside a hospital, whether ten doctors could've saved him. However, George was miles away from any hospital or anyone at all for that matter, and so it was here that George's life comes to its sad end.

We should be clear about this before we go any further because the terrible things that are about to happen are not George's fault. George was a good man, and we should remember him as such. Keyboard warriors and pithy flatulence ridden do-gooders will want to tarnish George's character, but we must not listen to them. We must seek wisdom and find out the terrible truth for ourselves. So, there in the dark lay George's lifeless body. His dogs now howling not just at the passing of their master but because of the encroaching stifling blackness.

There in the dark something shivered like a shadow wavering in slow motion. The dogs did not notice at first but soon sensed its presence. It shuddered like a sail on a boat or a sheet on a clothesline. The dogs had stopped howling now and had started growling. There in the impenetrable dark, the shape began to move. Such slow and such small movements even the dogs barely would've noticed in daylight. The shape was moving closer to George's dead body. When it got there, had we had the terrible displeasure of witnessing this event, we would have seen it hover over George's body just for a moment. Then the dogs noticed something. George moved. His lifeless body now resuming a standing position like a doll, or a puppet held by strings. The dogs started whining in fear and cowered away from its presence.

It spoke. "Get moving!" The voice wasn't like George's voice. It was a strange rasping voice with a very old-fashioned accent. With authority it gruffly spoke its command to the dark and George's body shuffled towards the entry of the tunnel. His face held no expression, and his eyes were soulless and grey. His dogs reluctantly followed, or at least two of his dogs did. The other was dead. They whined in the direction of their lost comrade. "Go" said the reanimated man. Leaving their mate behind and obviously fearful, the dogs obeyed and followed their new master back to the bus stop. As they came aboard the bus once again for the return journey, the bus driver ignored George's blank stare and odd movements. It was all too well that he did.

Earlier that day a middle-aged, olive-skinned couple, maybe even Punjabi? and a handsome young man in his mid-twenties, had just disembarked at Anderson International Airport. They had finished their long journey connecting El Anil to New Anderson but unlike flights of today, the comfort of even a third-class passenger was outstanding in 1982. One could be sure to arrive at your destination refreshed and well fed, or boozed. As the airplane spewed its passengers out into the warmth of the terminal, dozens of virgin tourists clamoured for the fascinating array of cleverly locally made bits 'n' bobs on sale in the little gift shops. Our troupe, however, totally ignored these distractions and bypassed them for the terminal's corridors that led to their connecting flight south (Doon). If one had been paying any attention to them, you might've noticed that the younger man was following the couple. Be that as it may, no one was noticing them at all. They seemed to just blend in with their surroundings and virtually disappeared into the canvas of the crowds moving from one place to the next. Had you been paying closer attention you might have seen the couple enter a cleaner's cupboard whilst the young man casually tried to act like he was not standing guard. Moments later, two thoroughly different individuals came out and the young man disappeared into the closet behind them. This time, and quite astonishingly, a small boy withdrew from the closet and greeted the two waiting for him. The boy was very average looking and not particularly handsome. His darker brown hair was a ruffle of uncertainty, and he gave the impression he was uncomfortable in his body. His eyes, on the other hand, could not disguise the brainpower he was so cleverly trying to conceal. He did seem rather pleased with himself though.

"'Tis a pleasure to make your acquaintance dear sir," the boy jested at the older man.

"Do so at your own peril young man" he replied. "These folks speak the common tongue and we had better imitate them as best we can".

The man spoke in a severe tone at the boy, but then his eyes glinted, and you could see there was great humour. The boy cheerfully punched the man's arm and retorted with a smile, "Come now! What foe lies in this here bedraggled village of peasants!" he guffawed to himself before reclaiming his composure.

"Let's be serious Eddie," aiming his speech towards both the boy and the woman. "The old man might not have told us everything yet." And so, the trio resumed their astounding task, with great skill it might be added, at blending into their environment.

1982, international flights all had to pass through New Anderson's capital city, which meant the new arrivals were still hours away from their destination. Eddie, Jack, and Mom made their way to the transit lounge and their departure gate for the connecting flight to Doon and there they waited. Eddie's cheerful mood did not last as he was already beginning to think overtime about all the possible awkward situations he would soon be thrust into now that he was a 10-year-old once again. His mind swam with the apprehension of the gawky social ineptitude he would feel at living amongst children again.

Many adults long to be children again, to be free of the burden of life's responsibilities and worries: to not care when the garden needs weeding or the hedge trimmed or getting the kids to their sports game on Saturday mornings. Eddie was, by nature, a deeply private soul who generally kept to himself and did not need to be in the company of others to feel cheerful. He loved forests and mountains and watching the Earth from high above as it turned. If he were being truly honest however, he would admit that he did greatly admire humans. Aside from their fanatical desire to murder each other, there was a trait in humankind that Eddie regarded highly. A significantly large portion of mankind kept a personal kind of faith. Not the kind of faith that must ritually do certain things to be 'good' but the kind that merely looked at the world and trusted its creator, all the while shrugging off the doubt that gnaws at the human soul with quite often simple logic. "If he says it's fine, then it's fine with me." That kind of faith impressed Eddie. It didn't need a show and that suited him to a tee.

Eddie was a shapeshifter as was Jack and Mom. That much must be undoubtedly obvious by now. They all had prodigious talents and each one had a special strength that set them apart from others like them. Eddie's skill was his ability to change his appearance, ranging anywhere from a small boy to a man in his mid-twenties. Jack had a similar ability but could make himself look much older and could morph his facial features to that of another ethnicity. Mom, of course, could shapeshift in much the same way as Jack, but, as you will discover, her talents were more than simply changing her appearance. Her magic was ostensibly the real reason they were all headed for Doon. Mom's talents were in what you would call the 'crazy boat' section of the local looney hospital. People like her were either mad or were not taken seriously at all. Mom, however, did not need to publish her work or be recognised, in fact the 'Committee' expressly forbade exposing any 'Shapeshifter' or their talents. It was the Committee's law that would undoubtably get Eddie into trouble.

Mom didn't share her specific power with anyone other than the Sharma and he knew well enough the gravity of the 'Vision' she had recorded. Her vision was not just about one person either, but, like all important visions, it centred around one person.

As with all magic, it was bounded by certain laws. Some of those laws were rules set in place by the elders of the 'Committee,' like the rule which prohibited the disclosure to any human, knowledge of their existence and purpose. Some rules could obviously be bent or even broken. Depending on the skill and power of a 'Member', they could surpass the known physical limitations of their powers. Take gravity for example. On Earth, gravity is remarkably consistent as is air or the speed of light. However, when you take gravity and commit massive amounts of energy and space to the equation, some of the rules begin to bend. Occasionally, even time itself can be warped by a truly colossal volume of focused, magical energy, but Eddie was yet to encounter a member who claimed to be adept at this. Powers like gravity and distance were all skills which any member had mastered before they were young adults, yet more specialised skills such as shapeshifting might take decades to fully master. Those that got it wrong could literally make a world of trouble for themselves, so it was for this reason that their concealment was closely protected by the Committee. And they were good at it. Particularly good at it.

They had been at work for thousands of years, so when you hear or see reports of mysterious supernatural events occurring, or maybe you hear of angels or demons wreaking havoc in a town somewhere, don't be alarmed. The Committee is very efficient at cleaning up its mistakes. There are from time to time, every century or so, events that occur in which even the Committee is alerted to investigate. Such events usually are so significant that the Committee will assign a team to examine and report back its findings. Is this the work of real angels? Or demons? We will not attempt to describe these for you now as we have our own events in this tale to explore.

Isolation from human society is dangerous, so members are expected to 'dwell' alongside certain people groups that the Committee deem to be 'of interest'. From time to time, members had discovered wild prophecies that were quickly consumed by the willing population. Sometimes they would be so farfetched they were actually true. Members would have to actively work to suppress certain details of these prophecies in order to stick to their plans. Maybe the Creator himself saw fit to intervene when events became too precarious? Eddie didn't think so but was nonetheless curious to find out. He had heard that Sharma had talked to an Angel, or was it that he had heard about one from someone else? He could not remember.

Eddie thought suspiciously at times that the Creator knew exactly what he was doing. Sometimes though, he didn't know whether to laugh or cry when he considered such things.

Emily didn't know whether to laugh or cry either. She had just witnessed that poor imp of a boy, Brent, attempt to jump the curb on his BMX bike and scare a young 1st year student. He had failed miserably and gone head over heels across the footpath and landed upside down in a flower bed. Emily was biting her tongue in dread or amusement; she couldn't be sure.

Brent hadn't hurt himself badly. He had some scratches and mostly it was his pride that was taking a beating. You could tell by the way his cheeks were a rosy colour and his eyes were almost scrunched up. By the time he had gathered himself together and got back on his feet, he could hear the shrieks of laughter from the other kids. One was very close to finding out how Brent liked to solve those sorts of embarrassing scenes. With his fists. he didn't get a chance though because luckily a grownup just happened upon the scene and, I might add, quite expertly diverted Brent's scrape away from the poor kid. How on earth Brent could go from an aggressive bully to a tearful victim in seconds was anyone's guess. Emily was shaking her head in disbelief when Eddie walked by her blissfully unaware of the debacle. He seemed quite happy to saunter past the incident and instead head for the school entrance.

"Hey, are you the new boy by any chance?" Emily called after Eddie as she hurried to catch up with him. "I think I might've seen you last night on your way home! You looked soaking wet, you poor thing you!"

Emily was clearly going to do all the talking, not letting Eddie get a word in at all.

"Umm, yeah I am." Eddie half chuckled in between Emily's tirade of pleasantness as they kept walking into school. The school itself wasn't quite as bad as Emily might have judged. It had some new classrooms and even a heated swimming pool. The courtyards and grounds were huge with plenty of room for kids to wander about and explore. The teachers were great but there was the odd one or two grumpy individuals who still liked to use corporal punishment. Many a kid would come back from the Vice Principal's office nursing a noticeably tender hand after receiving the 'belt' for some unjustified crime against education. Kids would often try their best to repress the desire to bawl as the pain of ridicule from the other kids was far worse than the physical pain inflicted by the belt. I still can't say whether Emily would ever admit to 'getting the belt' but I suspect not. Even in 1982 some teachers were still perfectly comfortable with disciplining girls and boys alike. Oh, how much has changed.

The south side of the school's campus was bordered by a small forest of trees with a path leading out towards the main road. If you liked exploring and playing fairy and hunting games, then this place would be a place of wonder for any child. Eddie was momentarily jerked from his silent musing by Emily making yet another comment. "I do hope you get put in my class," she said after finding out which year he was in. "Miss Beadle is an old wort but she'll make you laugh." Emily snorted out a giggle.

He didn't answer, but politely nodded and veered in the direction of the school office. Eddie had a distinct feeling he was going to see her again soon enough.

Emily was delighted when, a short while later, the school principal brought Eddie to her class and introduced him. He looked particularly aloof and detached. Emily thought Eddie didn't want to be there at all. He seemed a darn sight more than just embarrassed to be introduced to a room full of snotty-nosed idiot children. It appeared more like the whole experience was irritating to him. He didn't bother looking at any of the kids but was quite polite to Miss Beadle which surprised most of the kids. I would like to say that the rest of the day was very exciting and full of witty repartees but no, Eddie was an expert at blending in and not being noticed. Heck, if there was a school fire alarm drill that day it would probably have taken hours before anyone asked where Eddie was. He was just well skilled in making himself invisible, even if not literally.

Days went by and eventually Emily lost interest in her new school mate. She was a talkative, bright delightful young girl and he was becoming part of her everyday scenery. At first, she thought he might be interesting, but he seemed to be an expert at diverting conversations or topics away from himself or making you feel a bit awkward for even talking to him.

She did think it strange when one day during break she asked him what he thought about the cricket. "Have you heard they are talking about leaving the Commonwealth, because of those bloody Caernarvon's ruining the cricket?" Emily loudly stated to a group of kids sitting around. Some of the children chuckled at this. Emily was angling to go off on another group discussion but so far no one was biting at the obvious bait for witty discussion, so she aimed a little higher.

"What do you think Eddie?" she cleverly directed the question to him. "Oh, that," he yawned. "Have the Lords taken another head again?" clearly Eddie wasn't even in the right century. "No silly!" she said, "The underarm bowl!" Emily's eyes appeared to pop in astonishment at Eddie's lack of knowledge on the recent test series.

Eddie just stared blankly back at her in the hope that she would give up her performance and direct her drama elsewhere. He wasn't going to be that lucky.

Emily was clearly ramping up for a long speech on why and how it was totally unjust, and the Caernavorn cricketers should all be sacked. Eddie just stared blankly. He had better do some homework on cricket - soon.

However, this was bad timing for Eddie. Brent had somehow managed to overhear this delicious morsel of hilarity and jumped on the opportunity to taunt them. He would delight in being able to ridicule both Emily and Eddie in one display of superiority. "Doesn't know his cricket, eh?" Brent gloated. "What a twerp!" Brent was clearly trying to get a rise out of Eddie. He would have to try harder.

"What're yer even asking him for?" Brent spat at Emily, "this half-breed donkey wouldn't know cricket if it hit him in the face. Would eee?" Brent spewed this retort towards Eddie. "Where do you come from anyway? Mars?" Brent was trying so desperately to be funny, drawing attention to Eddie's different skin colour. By now Brent was having the time of his life, running high on the adrenalin surging inside. He hoped that soon he would get a chance to punch this stupid new kid who ignored him so well.

Brent was going to be disappointed. In fact, Brent was getting rather ruffled by now because his witty lines had produced nothing from either Eddie or Emily. Although a few interested kids were now milling around in the hope for a display of Brent's hunger for violence.

Next Brent tried pushing Eddie to see if he could get a reaction. Eddie had an enormous capacity for self-control and so Brent was once again on the verge of another disappointing anti-climax to his underwhelming display of sarcastic humour. Eddie wasn't even paying him attention at all, and to Brent's frustration, began to yawn. Emily opened her mouth to start her own witty repartee in response to Brent but was cut short just as Brent's fist was about to start towards Eddie's face.

"Stop that!" shouted the Vice Principal. "You've been warned Master Brent!" Now speaking directly to Brent. "We shall see what comes about, for those that play folly with my school rules young boy!" The teacher was absentmindedly touching his belt on his trousers. A few kids who saw this recognised immediately what it meant and the look on Brent's face revealed to all the fear now striking like a blow across his cheek.

As the Vice Principal led Brent off towards his office by the scruff of the poor boy's neck, Eddie looked on with disdain. "There's no stopping some people" he muttered to himself. Emily shot a glance at Eddie when she heard him. "Yeah," she declared self-righteously, "that Brent can't help himself!" Emily tried desperately now to gain some moral advantage over the situation. She was surprised, however, when Eddie, for once, responded to her.

"I didn't mean Brent," remarked Eddie coldly. Emily, taken aback, realised that Eddie was referring in fact to the Vice Principal. She was quite shocked at Eddie and more, so she was perplexed by his cryptic response to her. Everyone knew Brent was a bully who also liked showing off, but no kids would ever dare speak out against the Vice Principal. That man was a scary imposing figure. He was an exceptionally well-dressed man for his career station and was often seen scowling down his long nose through his bi-focal lens at the poor students of his school. Eddie said nothing. He was already making his way toward the school office.

Not much later, a sheepish Brent and a quiet Eddie were returned to class. Brent looked terrible and all the kids would have been thinking by now that he had been the recipient of the Vice Principal's penchant for corporal punishment. Eddie, as always, was simply dead pan. Not revealing anything was his forte. Eddie had done something very peculiar. He had petitioned the Vice Principal in spectacular style not to discipline Brent and argued that the fracas did not merit any punishment as it was merely a misunderstanding. How he'd been able to convince the Vice Principal to not give Brent's hands a good drubbing, was unfathomable.

This did little to alleviate the tension between Brent and Eddie, however. One could say that Brent now disliked Eddie even more than before.

"What did you do?" Emily whispered to Eddie. Emily was bursting with curiosity. She could hardly contain her urge to aim a dozen questions at him. Such was her inquiring mind, a few of the questions that darted across her mind were: "Did he get the strap?" Brent, that is. "Why was Eddie being so coy?" and "Did Eddie get Brent into even more trouble than he already was?" she thought to herself, her gaze darting from Brent and back to Eddie. Eddie just winked at her. This was perhaps the most communication she had ever enjoyed with Eddie since she had first met him. Her face was awash with the genuine surprise of his silent yet candid reply.

The next day Emily pressed Eddie again.

Eddie didn't seem bothered by her though. He just smiled. She was a wonder to him and even though she was making a legitimate case, he appreciated her boldness. He remained resolute; he would not talk about the debacle with her or anyone. Inwardly, Eddie was impressed by Emily. He had not met many girls like her and her curiosity and compassion seemed to be fighting for dominance over her personality. Regardless, Eddie found it hard to disappoint her.

He shrugged. "I don't really want to talk about the 'VP', Emily, or Brent for that matter." Eddie hoped that she would drop it.

There was silence for a moment. Eddie was not in a hurry to try and fill the air with meaningless chatter and Emily had sensed already that it would be pointless to try to push Eddie for an answer anyway.

Emily was already a million miles ahead and didn't see the sense in battering the poor guy. Besides, she liked Eddie even though he was so different. Maybe they just needed to hang out and have some fun together. School was no fun for Eddie, she could tell that a mile away, and he didn't seem to have made many friends either.

"Hey," she said playfully, "did you want to come up to the old castle with me and Mom this weekend? It's REEEEEEAL super old and creepy!

"I'll bet you haven't seen the old castle. Some believe it's haunted, you know" she said winking at Eddie.

"Of course, I don't BE-LEEEEEVE in magic and all that tosh." she kept going. "I'll bet you don't fall for any of that magic silliness either, do you?" Emily goaded him.

"Haunted you say?" asked Eddie, mocking Emily. "I shall be expecting the grand 'ghost tour' then my dear!' Eddie put on a terribly forced royal accent and held his fingers up like speech marks.

"Oh, do bring the carriage around to the servant's entrance about 'eightish', Charles dear!" Emily replied, bursting into laughter at Eddie's unexpected attempt at humour.

So, Eddie agreed, and accepted Emily's offer of a haunted castle tour and they arranged that Emily's mum would take them on Saturday. Emily told Eddie what she had heard about the girl who'd lived in the castle many years before.

"A girl died there apparently, and she never left the castle. Her rich dad had built the castle so he could see his business in the city through a telescope from the first storey window. I heard that he was so sad when she died that he left and never returned and eventually the whole estate had to be auctioned off, or something like that.

"They say her soul haunts the castle because she was waiting for her dad to return, and he never did."

Emily was a little hazy on the real facts.

"You know, for someone who doesn't believe in magic you seem to know a LOT about it Emily?" Eddie taunted her playfully.

"Nah, I don't believe in ANY of it!" she replied defiantly.

"I can't believe that anyone would!" she added, "but you and I are gonna have a brilliant time exploring round the castle Eddie!"

Emily was right. They had a fabulous time climbing up the tower, mock dancing in the ballroom, trying to turn the old butter churn and generally running all over the amazing grounds. The gardens weren't in the best condition, but they managed to make their way down to where the original owner had fashioned a gap in the trees and an area you could sit and view the entire city almost in one view. It was a stunning panorama from high up on the hill where they sat.

Eddie remembered when he'd first arrived in Doon and had looked up to the far-off hill above the town and wondered what was up there. Now he knew. There weren't any strange foreboding mysteries left hidden in this town, he thought to himself. There'd just been an old rich guy whose daughter died, and it broke his heart, so he abandoned his castle. People always made-up stories of 'magic' and angels and such to make boring heart-breaking stories more entertaining and mysterious. For what purpose? He wondered.

Later, as they returned home from the castle, they passed Chippenham's chicken farm on their way down the hill. As they neared the gate to the farm, they noticed a small gathering of people milling round. Like in all small communities, within 5 minutes of something happening you can guarantee that most housewives have found out about it, making it virtually impossible to keep a secret. So, for Pam it was her duty to stop and make enquiries as she hated the idea of hearing from someone else later. As she slowed her car, Emily's mum spotted Constable Matt Ferguson talking with the farmer and a local car salesman, deep in a heated discussion about something, and they hadn't noticed Pamela's car glide up beside them.

The car salesman recognised Pamela as a neighbour of his yard manager.

"Ahem," he coughed a little too noisily to be mistaken for anything other than to alert the others they had company. "Hello Pam!" Sam beamed a big smile at her.

"Hello kids! Been up to no good I hope," he joked, leaning his head in the window to beam his great big ugly salesman smile at Eddie and Emily. Sam, being an expert in people relations made sure everyone was introduced. "Pam, you know Constable Matt an' John Chippenham don'tcha?"

"Hi Sam." Pam nodded to the constable and the farmer.

"Farmer's in a bit of a pickle, ya see. Some of his chickens gone missin'an' we found a couple dead along the road a wee bit with dere heads wrung out. Matt here reckons it might be some young scallywags that live nearby."

The farmer shot a serious look at Sam. They ALL knew who Sam was talking about.

"Brian and a couple of his mates having a bit of 'fun' is one thing," said Matt earnestly, "but we can't rush to conclusions just yet." He eyed the farmer with intense scrutiny. He wasn't about to let Brian get taken into custody for just being accused of killing chickens. They'd have to hope something came up in the next 'wee' while. He didn't want a chicken killer on the loose now did he. Matt chuckled to himself "God, what has the world come to? We've got a lone chicken strangler out there somewhere......"

"Killing chickens is a bit mad, isn't it?" Pamela chipped in. "I've never heard of it." Emily was making clucking noises in the back trying to get Eddie to mimic her but was having no success. Eddie was captivated by the strange story of a chicken killer. He was trying to hear what the farmer was saying over Emily's mimicry.

"Well lad, that'll have to be proven but I can tell you it sure as hell weren't dogs!" John the farmer was raising his voice now. "Dogs don't wring chickens' necks, do they?"

"I'll tell ya what I did find strange, lad" he paused.

"Well, probably not stranger than me chickens bein' taken but definitely weird by all accounts, lad." Pausing for more dramatic effect, John lent in towards Matt and whispered to the constable. "Last night I had to chase the old man George's dogs off my driveway."

Matt looked perplexed. He had never heard of any complaints about the old man's dogs or anything at all about the grumpy old man for that matter. He had, however, heard many complaints about that young idiot Brian. He only hoped he was wrong. He knew Brian's mum and dad well enough and from what Sam and John had just said, he was beginning to wonder if they were right.

John was being a bit dramatic about the whole shenanigans, thought Matt. But he knew that if it were Brian, or one of his mates, then pretty soon they'd be bragging about it down at the local pub and his work would be mostly done for him. For now, though, he was content to enjoy the show and let the two older men feel they were running the investigation. People liked that, thought Matt, and it amused him sometimes the sense of self-importance it seemed to give people. Or at least he thought it did.

If Eddie had known what Matt was thinking, he would've wholeheartedly agreed and slapped him on the back, possibly even buying the young policeman a pint of beer for his good sense. But Eddie was a 10-year-old boy and could not read minds, so from his perspective he thought all three of them were self-absorbed old twats standing there not really achieving anything at all. He did happen to think that Matt seemed to be the only sensible one though. Eddie was finding the whole situation quite amusing, so when Pamela announced they were 'off' because they had to get Eddie home, he was a bit disappointed.

Emily was still trying to get Eddie to mimic a dead chicken. At least someone found the chicken thing funny, he thought. He was glad that they had become friends.

Emily stopped her dead chicken dance and stared at Eddie for a while.

"Why the sad face, Ed?' she asked him. Eddie was oblivious to the fact he was deep in thought and Emily had mistaken his deep concentration for something else. He was in fact wondering if he should query Jack as to whether they had ever heard of random chicken killings back in Isin. Then, realising how preposterous the idea was, he laughed out loud at its absurdity.

"You know," said Eddie, "it's more likely someone got out of the local looney hospital and killed those chickens, I reckon.

"Ish wass meee, I killl all dem chikennnnns! I want more! gimme more!" Eddie did his worst impersonation of a mental patient.

Laughing at Eddie, Emily realised even though he was quite different to the other kids, he was fun and safe. He didn't mock and make fun of her, belittling her just because she was smart.

Pam had noticed it too and all the way home they chatted about this and that and where they might take Eddie to explore next time they had a free weekend.

Emily was glad she had asked him to the castle. She hoped they would become good friends.

CHAPTER 02
DISCOVERY

It was almost Christmas in 1982 and Eddie had well and truly settled in to his new 'school'. Emily's life hadn't changed much, and her father didn't look like returning anytime soon either. Eddie had fully achieved his goal of 'blending' in the environment and was hardly being noticed. He was still the loner but because his house was so close to Emily's, he very often wound-up walking with Emily after school. Emily liked walking with Eddie, he wasn't like the other kids and wasn't intimidated by her propensity for 'going off' on often random discussions. Sometimes the 'discussions' were about the social injustice of girls not being allowed to play on the cricket team, or it was why kids weren't supposed to ask questions of adults (this one she would get particularly agitated about).

"I mean, what's the point?" she would argue. "If you can't ask decent questions? And why do the grown-ups tell me to shut my 'cake-hole' all the time? I wish they would shut their 'cake' holes!" Emily stated earnestly. Eddie was entertained by her debates. She was right though, even Eddie was aggravated by the way adults treated him at times.

Emily loved being able to talk to someone who was on her level he wasn't prone to making silly criticisms like other kids. The 'other' kids would jeer at her statements and try to make fun of her. This hurt Emily (like it would any young girl) but she knew deep down they were just jealous of her. Eddie, on the other hand, loved the conversations they had. He would sometimes chuckle at her quaint local colloquialisms. "She'll be right" was one of his favourites. Or, "Put a sock in it". He found that one particularly amusing.

Emily continued her monologue, "It's as if they are afraid to be wrong at all! It's so irritating!" she would exclaim severely. This was much of the reason why many girls her age weren't inclined to be her buddies or 'bffs'. Perhaps to them, she wasn't interested in Barbie enough or maybe it was because she was a bit forthright and brusque. Most of the time even grownups don't handle overly blunt people, they're just more polite about it. Emily acted like she didn't care, but secretly she hated the way the girls treated each other. They were so catty and bent on criticising the most ridiculous things. "Who cares if Betty has pigtails and a slight rash on her face?" Emily would argue to herself. Truth is that most young people are so immature they don't notice the hurt of others. Emily wasn't like 'most' other kids. She noticed alright, and it made her blood boil at times.

December in Doon wasn't like the rat race to Christmas as in some other places. In Doon it was a gentle affair that thankfully didn't have all the unnecessary marketing campaigns and billboards endlessly recommending useless toys to parents who couldn't afford to buy them anyway. You probably wouldn't even realise it was almost holidays. Back then, people didn't cover their houses in expensive lighting displays, and you weren't perpetually seeing advertisements everywhere telling you what your neighbour (most likely wealthier than you) would be buying for Christmas. Emily did ever so wish for a new cassette tape player (her dad had left a Bill Collins tape behind, and she loved it) and not a new Barbie doll like most other girls her age. She would often prefer to take her gumboots and (on a good day) walk out to the estuary and look for shells for hours. Nothing could have bored her more than to play make-believe with a party of girly dolls.

Sometimes the only way you could tell it was nearing 'that' time of year was the Redemption Brigade (the local religious temple) trucks with their brass bands playing carols or the local temple choirs singing beautifully crafted arrangements of the tunes we love at Christmas time. Emily enjoyed the carols and the music, even if it did remind her that her dad wouldn't be home for Christmas. She had not admitted it to Eddie though, it would be no use as Eddie wasn't exactly forthcoming when it came to discussing matters of the heart. I guess, like most boys his age, he was adept at being socially awkward when it came to expressing his feelings or acknowledging the emotions of others. Eddie was either truly a superb actor or he was naturally gawky.

Often, as they walked together, Emily would do most of the talking and Eddie would listen. He was a genuinely superb listener and didn't just pretend to listen either. Every now and then he would interject with a comment or a funny quip at her seemingly self-righteous moral views. Today was no exception. They had just been at the little convenience store near the bus turnaround at the top of the rise and using her weekly allowance, Emily had purchased a lolly packet for 10 cents. It was a huge treat for Emily, but she kindly offered some sweets to Eddie. As they made their way back (probably arguing what colour wine gum was the best choice), to the top of Every Street, Emily was suddenly startled by Brent and a couple of his friends who were obviously all bored and looking for trouble. She had been oblivious to them and deep into explaining how the orange lollies weren't orange flavoured at all. Eddie was fully engrossed in this entertaining debate and hadn't seen the boys race towards him and Emily either.

The pesky bunch of punks had achieved their objective of spooking Emily but had had absolutely no effect on Eddie whatsoever. I won't say that Emily 'shrieked' in alarm, but it was reasonable to assume that she said something loudly involving a couple of four-letter words that mum had said she should never use. Scared, she reacted quite out of character and took off down a steep (dead-end) lane heading along the opposite side of the hill towards the lagoons and past the farm. It was a silly thing to do as the boys could easily make chase on their bikes and trap her at the bottom of the steep lane. There was a tall hedge on either side, and it didn't look anything like an escape route, in fact, it appeared rather menacing and dark. It is sort of amusing to analyse the kind of things we do when we react in fear. Eddie quickly followed Emily as the boys all laughed cynically at their triumph. For a few moments, it looked like the boys would abandon the chase since they seemed to be satisfied with their endeavours - and it's a bit scary even for a tough 10-year-old to ride down a steep narrow lane when you don't know what's at the end and you must consider walking back up again later.

"Yeah, run away little girls!" shouted Brent and the boys all laughed again. Brent's hopes that the pair might take his bait were dashed as they ran (quite dangerously and a bit too fast) down the lane. If you've ever had the displeasure of falling over whilst running fast down a hill, then you will empathise (and perhaps grimace) with the poor soul who makes such a mistake. Eddie and Emily were lucky that this didn't befall them on this occasion, and they made it to the end of the lane quite fast but needed to let the farm gate stop them at the bottom. It was also fortuitous for them that the gate had no barbs to cut their hands on. They almost crashed into each other as the pair hit the gate quite a bit harder than they expected but they'd made it there before the boys and so jumped across into the steep paddock beyond. The boys chasing them almost had a pileup of their own and barely managed to avoid it. They started fighting each other as they rose to begin blaming each other for causing an incident.

"Moron! Didn't you see I'm in the front?!" Brent shouted at one of the boys.

"My, my... my b,b,b brakes aren't very good!" stammered the other boy, clearly a bit intimidated by Brent.

"Well now we'll have to w, w, w, w, walk back up, won't we?" the older boy said sarcastically mocking the younger kid.

They soon gave up their shouting at each other and realised that Eddie and Emily had escaped. "I'm not chasing after those losers anyway," said Brent. "Farmer Duncan knows my dad. If he sees us, he'll be sure to tell him, right?" Brent reasoned quite well but I think neither Brent nor the boys really felt like leaving their bikes and chasing off down into the farm anyway. It's a shame really because had they followed the pair, their adventure might've ended much differently.

Emily stopped running shortly after and she and Eddie soon observed that no one was following them down into the paddock.

Sprinting away in surprise had left the pair quite excited and full of nervous energy. Their elation at escaping Brent and his 'loons' was bubbling to the surface and Emily started laughing, which made Eddie start to snicker too.

"Hey!" said Emily excitedly. "Do you wanna see the lagoon?" "You haven't seen it right?" she asked inquisitively. "I'll bet there's some cool exploring down there," she tried to convince Eddie, but he didn't need much persuasion at all.

"I'm keen" he asserted in reply, a smile forming on his face. Since he had arrived in Doon, his 'exploring' had been hampered by Jack's rule and even 'Members' couldn't see in the dark. So, the pair took off like vintage explorers seeking out a new adventure in undiscovered country. They would've looked like a couple of kids trespassing private property the way they kept glancing nervously back up the hill every few moments, because that's exactly what they were. Eddie and Emily soon made it through the woods bordering the lagoon and reached the large patch of tall reeds which almost covered the shallow water. The topmost lagoon drained into another bigger lagoon just below it so that after a few weeks without rain you could almost walk across the lagoon and jump from one cluster of reeds to the next.

"This should be fun," he said, getting a genuine reply of surprise from Emily.

"Yeah!" agreed Emily. "It sure beats fighting those losers up there anyway. God, I do wish that idiot Brent would grow up!" Emily declared. But she wouldn't let Brent ruin a perfectly good excuse to explore the lagoon nor would she let him dampen her spirits either.

"Who knows what cool stuff is down here anyway," Eddie said, trying to divert his mind from the temptation to keep looking back up the hill just in case Brent and his 'gang' had changed their mind.

"I wouldn't worry about that chump!" Emily said. "He's far too lazy to come on a real adventure".

Soon it would be getting dark as even in December sunset was still unwelcomely early (usually dinner time for Emily) and on the shadow side of the hill the temperature and light had dropped dramatically since they'd been there. I don't know for sure if it was the change in sunlight or the excitement of the new surroundings but Eddie somehow managed to clumsily lose his balance when jumping from one clump of reeds to the next. Emily (always in front) had just turned to witness him fall into the cold dirty water.

This time, she did let out a loud shrill squeal. Her hands rose to cover her face in fear or horror (or disbelief?) at what she saw.

Eddie had changed, only for a few moments of course, but that would be enough for anyone as observant as Emily. For a moment, as he flailed in the frigid water (and in shock himself), he held the appearance of a handsome man in his mid-twenties. His large shoulders on his tall lean frame made him appear bigger and his sudden unshaven face now a shock of worry and tension mixed with chagrin. Eddie was clearly bewildered by both his blunder at falling into the lagoon but also at Emily's reaction.

As she backed away apprehensively from Eddie (now clambering out of the water as fast as he could), she was becoming more upset, and Eddie had now realised something much darker and more ominous must have frightened Emily. It didn't take him too long to figure out it was he who had scared her.

"What are you? Who are you? What WAS that?!!" Emily blurted out.

As she backed away, however, she tripped over some grass and fell into the water herself.

"Oh great!" muttered Eddie sarcastically, "it HAS to get worse, doesn't it?!" he declared, looking upwards at the sky in mute appeal to no-one.

Emily was flailing herself now. Falling into frigid water at the bottom of a valley on the other side of the hill from your home when it's just about to get dark, is not the best recipe for a successful exploring adventure. Emily was shaking and shivering from the cold and hysteria was beginning to claw at her consciousness Now sudden waves of fear were amplified by the decreasing temperature and her powerlessness at coping with it. As Eddie struggled to help pull Emily out of the water, her face was a jumble of confusion. Eddie was the 10-year-old boy she stared at in disbelief now.

"Was I imagining it?!" she blurted out, almost to herself. "Who, or w, w, w, wh, what was th, th that?" she shivered the words out slowly.

Eddie had gathered his thoughts by now and his stern face was masking his own fears. He was torn between saving the poor girl from what would undoubtably be exposure or escaping to the relative safety of his home, which would mean abandoning her to the cold. You see, when a person experiences the hazards of being wet and extremely cold at the same time, often even a strong adult has trouble keeping their mind focused and ready to react assertively. Emily had never experienced anything like it, so her mind was swimming, and she was going into shock. Eddie would have to choose fast and, more importantly, he would have to act. Soon.

So, taking great risk and absent-mindedly biting his lip nervously (or was it the cold?) he picked Emily up and jumped. Well, kind of. The mere fact a 10-year-old boy could pick up a soaking wet girl let alone 'jump' with her is not just almost physically impossible, it's also absurd! He did it though. He picked her up in his arms and jumped.

And disappeared. Quite literally was there one moment and then gone the next, but within moments they arrived sopping wet in the entrance of Eddie's house. Miraculously and virtually instantaneously, they'd gone from the lagoon to the other side of the hill and inside Eddie's house in a matter of seconds.

Mom was standing there. A severe look on her face of both worry for Emily and disdain for Eddie.

"Eddeeeee!" she cackled in her typically strange mixture of accents. "yousszz better haff a being in hheeer! Mhar achshio" she unconsciously babbled at Eddie in some foreign tongue. Mom was a very matronly looking figure of sternness and loving kindness all kneaded up in the melting pot of her expressions. Mom seemed like any mom in her mid-forties. An apron around her skirt and her hair all tied up in what looked distinctly like a tea towel! Had Emily bothered to look at Mom, she would have noticed something slightly different about her eyes, but she was shaking and shivering with the cold and the shock.

Inside the house, however, it was warm and smelled like a marvellous combination of freshly baked bread and coffee and the hint of meat cooking (was it roast lamb and mint?). Mostly Emily was experiencing the generous warmth of the unnaturally oversized and magnificent room with the richly carpeted floor they were now dripping onto. "You's a poor theeng eh!" said Mom putting a towel and an arm around Emily's shoulders whilst leading her away.

Since Emily was still shocked and suffering from the effects of exposure to the cold, she couldn't possibly have taken it all in and besides, Mom was far too quick and had bustled her up the stairs to get her changed into dry clothes but not without aiming a frank command to Eddie. "Be prepared to answer for this Eddeee" Mom said as she turned her head towards Eddie, who was having a difficult time reading the worried expression on her face. Was it anger? Dread? Was it genuine unfiltered panic he had seen in her expression? He didn't know. His own mind was even struggling to stay focused, and he hadn't noticed up until now that his body was shaking.

Groaning, Eddie knew the gravity of his decision to 'jump' both himself and Emily to safety. He had broken two rules and one of them was profoundly serious. Not that Jack or even Mom would disagree with his judgement, but Eddie would need to have a darn good explanation and not just to them. The Sharma would demand an answer as would the 'Committee'. The Sharma he could handle but Eddie had not been tested by many senior Members and had good reason to be considerably apprehensive as to what to expect. His willingness to assist Emily was of course truly compassionate and caring, but nonetheless extremely daring. Many of the possible scenarios that were bouncing around his head were all fraught with danger of some kind. He would not have a sensible answer to give for breaking their most absolute rule (law?).

Eddie wasn't just trembling from the cold now. He fought to contain himself and focus his troubled mind. It is no easy task to do such a thing. Excitement and fear send out powerful chemicals and your body surges with false emotional knee-jerk reactions that can make you behave quite out of character.

Thankfully, he was not alone. Jack had quietly entered the room from downstairs and even though it must have been painfully obvious to him the predicament they were in; he calmly laid his hand on Eddie's shoulder. Eddie started at first (he was still trying to get a hold of himself) then succumbed to the older man's assertive but consoling grip and managed to relax, albeit in small increments. Jack muttered something to the air.

"astki ms krim ozerot" he said quietly in a foreign language. "Awir oachum hroach." The room fell silent, and Eddie once again relaxed while Jack continued his utterances.

As Jack spoke, Eddie's clothes became dry, and his warmth returned. The colour came back to Eddie's face as did the determination to explain his mess. Jack ever so calmly raised his hand to stop Eddie.

"Eddie, there is time for that, but it is not now. Now you must eat and rest. Neither Mom nor I will judge you for this". Jack's voice was soft and quiet but held much weight.

Eddie heaved a sigh. He was relieved of course, and Jack was right. There would be time for explanations soon enough. Their chief task now was to make sure Emily was going to be ok. Not to mention that by this time Pamela would be anxious to know her daughter's whereabouts let alone if she was OK. As fortune would have it, Pamela knocked on the door. Jack answered it.

"Is Emily there?" she asked Jack. 'it's not like her to be late home but I understand if those kids have been playing" she mused. "I like Emily to have good company," she wasn't going to let Jack get a word in. "Emily really likes hanging with Eddie," she stated with a broad smile, trying to impress as much as possible.

"Yes Pamela, Emily and Eddie are playing upstairs in our study." he lied. "I can call them down now if you like." Jack didn't seem to be the slightest bit concerned about Pamela or the recent afternoon's events.

"Oh no! Don't bother them on my account," she replied graciously. "Emily can stay for a while if she wants. It's just," (she hesitated awkwardly) I have to rush to the airport to pick up my aunt on the 8pm arrival and I'm not sure that Bun likes the journey much."

Jack was quick. "Pick her up on your return if you so desire". He offered blandly, expertly hiding his concern like a master poker player.

It is not uncommon to find oneself being in these farcical situations where two parents try to 'out-do' each other in a battle of feigning graciousness. One parent tries desperately to be more congenial and polite, and it usually ends with one surrendering to the other's onslaught of niceness by reluctantly accepting their benevolent offer with mock humility. Neither is the winner, and both exit feeling like they have traded a worthless commodity for nil reward. Those who perform these tasks with cunning precision are worthy of Academy Awards or a local recognition of their superior acting skills at least.

Jack was a natural. He, however, had the distinct advantage of being several hundred years older than Pam and was a clever master of his facial expressions. Pamela had been offered a choice that was too good to turn down though and was visibly flustered. She certainly didn't have time to play the awkward game of polite to-and-fro with Jack, so she cordially agreed to return later that evening.

As Emily's mum was making her 'goodbyes' and 'see-you-laters' on her exit, Eddie was picking at a bowl full of nuts, his visage clearly relieved by the way Jack had skilfully averted another disaster. Jack's and Eddie's eyes met for the first time since Eddie's sudden return. Eddie felt the weight of the world on his shoulders. The responsibility, the fault, the crisis was all his fault, and it was crushing him. He would need a lot more than a gentle pat on the shoulder to ease his burden, but he was grateful to Jack for not judging him too soon. He didn't have much time to get himself together, soon Emily would return from upstairs and would want answers. He was acquainted with her well enough now to know she would need a rational explanation for the day's events. It was a conundrum for sure. If they refused and told her she had just knocked her head or something similar, then they would be risking her possibly not believing them. Equally problematic, was the danger of Emily befalling the same outcome even if they did 'disclose' the truth to her. Of course, that was all depending on whether Emily would, or even could, accept the truth about who they were.

Never, however, had Eddie felt such enormous compassion for an 'adami' (this was the name they conferred upon humans). To him it seemed profoundly unjust to inflict a future on a mere girl who would be ridiculed for the rest of her life for believing in angels or 'shapeshifters'.

"Eddie!" Emily called to him. He abruptly jerked from his deep deliberation and faced Emily with an honest face, once again a vision of calm and ready to do what was needed.

"I know what you are, Ed" Emily declared now fearlessly. "And, I'm....... I'm..."

Emily faltered. Her eyes a mixture of worry and awe as she tried hard to contain her weak emotional state. Like all girls, she thought it was her fault and had somehow deserved to be reprimanded for her ignorance.

"I'm sorry I was such a mug back there!" she confessed meekly. "I was a pig, wasn't I?" Emily was on the verge of tears.

"No, Emm." Eddie replied with certainty now, trying as hard as he possibly could to convey an expression of caring and kindness. "It's my fault. I shoulda...."

He didn't get to finish. Emily had wrapped her arms around him and hugged him tightly. Eddie hadn't realised how much Emily might have desperately needed his humble acknowledgment of her feelings. Both were genuinely taken aback.

"My mum says things are meant to be," Emily said between her tears. "And you probably saved my life down there Ed!" She was exaggerating now. It was an emotional rollercoaster for Emily. Eddie, Jack, and Mom seemed to let Emily react in her own way. They couldn't (or perhaps they refused to) try to manipulate her reactions to favour them.

"You're a Shapeshifter aren't you, Ed?" she questioned. "And Jack and your mom are too, right?"

"That's how you changed, isn't it?" Emily was picking up speed now, soon she would be asking the really important questions.

Neither Eddie nor Jack felt like answering immediately. Mom interjected in her usual manner.

"eet iss nawht to be told, ye must be shown child" she spoke to Emily in her unusual accent. Mom did not wait for Emily's response apparently oblivious.

"ish laroth at ahazon" Mom spoke to the air as if addressing an invisible guest. Mom was going to get carried away and Emily was already frowning in confusion at Mom's difficulty with language. It needn't have mattered anyway because a vision appeared to Emily, a sort of holographic representation of someone in a dream, and as Mom muttered her chant-like hymn Emily saw in front of her a scene that she recognised instantly. It was of her, that much was obvious. It was of Emily falling into the water. A look of vexation flushed Emily's face as she saw herself in such a state. Emily didn't have time to react or reflect on the embarrassing recollection she was gazing at. The vision changed and Emily now saw a much older woman standing in what looked like a gallery. It was an important gallery with important people wearing important clothes all sitting or standing in rows of important looking seats. Emily gazed at the woman (in her late thirties perhaps?) and instantly recognised her. It was her! It was Emily, a much older Emily mind you and she had a stern face of grim determination. Emily couldn't catch the words the older version of herself spoke, but Emily could discern from the face that she was issuing a mighty rebuke to someone. Emily was eager to hear what the words were and the person she was addressing. She wouldn't however, because the vision had ended, and the room was back to normal and none of the people in the room would offer such an interpretation to her anyway.

Eddie was stunned silent by the incredulity of the vision he had witnessed and even more amazed at Moms hidden powers of foresight.

Emily didn't know whether to be appalled by this amazing and stunning show of power or thoroughly impressed. Emily chose neither. I imagine anyone (let alone a child) would be close to or already hysterical by now and so Emily's response was reassuring to Jack, Mom, and Eddie. That Emily wanted answers was problematic but at least she wasn't panicking and for a 10-year-old she really was quite level-headed to decide on the wiser option. So, for the next hour or so Eddie, Jack and occasionally Mom told Emily what and who they were. Eddie told her that he was about 468 years old and that was young compared to Jack and Mom. Mom didn't really need to show much more as her vision was so credible and believable already. Beforehand, whilst they were upstairs getting her dry, Emily had started to notice the things around her. The magnificence of the interior decorating and the sheer brilliance of the rooms couldn't be missed even in her current state of mind. Emily did find it hard to believe such a house could exist on their street full of run-down state houses. "Even the bathroom is warm!" she had thought to herself. "I'll bet no one has a warm bathroom in all New Anderson!" Emily had whistled to herself in wonder.

Jack explained that whilst they had some supernatural gifts and skills, they had limitations. Eddie could only jump a few miles and had even taken a risk jumping with Emily. "Were not Angels or Demons, Em...." he pointed out, noticing the concerned look Emily was giving him. "But whatever we do, we do to save 'adami' from annihilating each other." He tried to explain but was having trouble deciding how much he should tell her. Telling Emily too much could be a dangerous business.

Even though Emily was told that they most certainly were not Angels or Demons, Jack strongly impressed on her to be very afraid if they should ever encounter one. You, as the reader, should know that Emily did not learn of why there were shapeshifters in Doon that night. Emily did not think to ask such a question. She regretted this later in life, but I think she knew even then that she would not get an answer to that question anyway. Emily was right in assuming very little disclosure from any of them, about their motives and intentions, but one thing she knew for sure: Eddie truly did care about her. He had proven that much to her and that was enough, for now.

"What happens if people find out what you are?" Emily asked, not realising it was probably the smartest question.

"That you have discovered who we are isbecause of who 'YOU' are Emily" explained Jack. "Whilst you say you don't believe in magic and Eddie doesn't believe in 'Fate', what has happened, has happened.

"What will be, will be!" interjected Eddie seriously.

"We can see that this was 'meant to happen now and no-one could have prevented it, neither could we have planned it," Jack took his time but felt that he should comfort Emily in case it was too much for her to absorb. He needed to be absolutely clear about one thing though.

“What matters the most is that no other human being learns of us or what you have witnessed today.” Jack spoke firmly but kindly to Emily.

“Ever,” he stressed. “Not even your own mother can know.” Jack was being wholly emphatic now.

“The risk is too great......” He paused to gather his thoughts.

“Ok, ok, okaaaaaaaaaaaaay!” Emily spoke sincerely. No doubt she meant it. What kid wouldn’t after hearing and seeing all that. The test for Emily would come over the next few days and months as to whether she could stand by her word. A terrible secret is a heavy thing to carry even for a grown adult! But for now, it seemed that Eddie, Jack, and Mom had given themselves no choice but to place their trust in a 10-year-old girl.

Eddie would’ve liked to have explained far more to Emily, but he was cut short by a knock at the front door.

“Is it that time already?” Eddie burst out impatiently. “She hasn’t got a chance!” Eddie exclaimed pleading to Jack. “Is there nothing we can do?!” He looked at Mom hopelessly.

As Jack went to answer the door, Mom addressed Eddie without delay.

“We will have hope in this child Eddeeee, she is special to us now!”

As Emily turned to go, she winked at Eddie. “it’s ok Ed, what could possibly go wrong?” she laughed at her attempt to break the tension. Eddie managed a wry smile and punched her playfully on the arm.

“Ha!” he replied, “who’d believe a couple of crazy kids talking about shapeshifters and angels anyway, eh?” Eddie almost broke into a grin and Emily returned his humour with a serious smile herself, before meeting her mum (quite shrewdly) in the entrance which just happened to be considerably larger than a few weeks before. They said their goodnights and ‘see you tomorrows’ quite awkwardly too, Emily trying her hardest to ‘underact’ and pretend that she wasn’t half as excited as she was. Eddie was relieved. He looked pleased with himself as he considered the night's catastrophe.

"Well, that could've been much worse, eh?" he said nervously as he fixed his stare on Mom's deeply troubled expression.

"Let us not be distressed 'ashti', we have done this before, remember?" Jack comforted Mom with his words.

"We shall hear from the old man soon enough," he stated knowingly. Jack had managed, as had Mom, to resist the urge to deliver an angry accusation at Eddie for his irresponsible actions. The rebuke never came. And so, they all faced the night's troubled sleep at least knowing their own house was at peace and that troubles, wherever they may be, can wait for another day.

That night Eddie slept peacefully despite the day's events. He had learned to trust his strange family and, like the Sharma had promised many decades before, his abilities were indeed growing stronger. He was even strangely at ease with Emily. Her response to his morphing had been naturally hysterical but later, when she had encountered the magic of the vision, her response to Eddie and Mom and Jack had been somewhat of a wonderful surprise. As he lay there in the dark listening to the great grandfather clock in the hall, it reminded him of his much earlier experience decades before, watching over another person special to him. The clock had a nostalgic effect as if by magic transporting him many decades in the past to the castles of Moray where he had lived. The great clocks were sometimes the only thing you might hear in the large corridors of the royal castles, and they had helped him get to sleep many a time. Even Emily, barely a few 100 yards away down the street, also felt unusually 'ok' about Eddie and the day's events. After dreamily wondering if she'd experienced a crazy delusion herself, Emily fell into a calm slumber, this time devoid of the violence and destruction she had dreaded dreaming again.

CHAPTER 03 ELDERS

The next few days were like a surreal dream for Emily as she came to terms with her recent experience and her new 'friends', albeit strange ones at that. Surreal, because our strange 'family' of shapeshifters were exceptionally skilled in acting 'normal'. Mom may have a strange accent and mannerisms that could be out of place in the state housing suburbs of Doon in 1982, but Mom was an expert. She was also very well acquainted with the age-old tradition of 'local' people speaking louder when talking to 'foreigners' as if somehow foreign people suffered from loss of hearing. It amused Mom greatly and she used her 'ignorance' to her advantage with the locals. Most people who lived here were descendants of the original Moray or Caernarvon settlers over 150 years ago. There was one Urudesh man who was a professor at the university, and he was married to a Morakin lady. There was a Xia'n couple who ran a local fish'n'chip shop down in the Mornington shops but other than that you would hardly ever see or hear 'foreign' people in the south at all. Even most of the indigenous Otene folk lived in the North, although there were a few settlements scattered here and there and the Moray had adopted many of the local Otene names for streets and places. Mom was a foreigner, yes, but because she stayed in the house 99% of the time, her impact on the outside world was very low. Jack and Eddie were fabulous at pretending to be the most utterly boring people you could ever not wish to meet.

Emily was astounded at Jack's skill in mimicking the locals.

"Eh up!" he would say to Eddie, laughing at his uncanny ability to master the accent. He especially liked the way the locals rolled their 'R's when they spoke. "I'm off down to Morrrrrington" he would say, overemphasising the 'R's with a big grin on his face.

If Emily was anxious about how she felt towards Eddie (and his parents), she didn't let it show. Remarkably she felt confident and comfortable in their company and even Mom's strange language at times wasn't alien to her. Emily was more fascinated by her than 'weirded out'. And when Emily got to stay for meals, she was treated to some of the most tantalising food she could've ever imagined possible. Not that the local cuisine was anything to rave about mind you. Most local folk ate lamb chops and boiled all their vegetables then mashed them up. Doon was hardly the most exciting culinary destination you could hope to visit, but people in the South didn't eat any differently because they didn't want to. No. It was decades of near almost poverty, harsh conditions and the lack of a vibrant local economy that stopped most from exploring tastier options from different cultures. People here were a stubborn bunch too and often you would hear "I don't go for that foreign muck! I'll be sittin' on the loo for days!". Most people would've considered fish'n'chips for dinner a superb treat. Emily really didn't care at all about mashed spuds and mutton chops, but she did love Mom's cooking and her odd mannerisms and language. It was exciting and new for Emily, and it suited her curious nature.

Emily's previously awkward distance from her mum, Pam, had almost all but disappeared and even though Emily had been witness to an extraordinary display of 'magic' (as she would fondly call it) she chose to hang out with her mum buying presents for all the cousins and aunts and uncles at the big Christmas dinner they were so looking forward to. They spent an enormous amount of time decorating their wee cottage together and it was a huge chance to heal for Emily being so close to her mum. Pam had taken the week off before Christmas to prepare for all the family that would visit over the coming weeks.

During this time, they also tidied up all of Wayne's clothes and belongings and carefully boxed them up and put them in the garage. Pamela might've felt abandoned and hurt by her husband leaving them, but she forced herself to do the right thing and respect what she considered as his 'belongings'. Having no idea if he would return was a burden on Pamela and she carried the weight of that for both her and Emily. Pam sometimes felt suffocated and anxious without Wayne around and a few times Emily caught her just staring out the window. However, Emily's "Hey Mum" was enough to pull her back from her temptation to dissolve in front of her daughter. If Pam had been left to her own defences and not had Emily to care for, she might have imploded. It was a benefit for both Pam and Emily that, as they sang Christmas carols whilst hanging decorations and buying Christmas treats for the family, it distracted them each from their own personal dilemmas. Pam had been insistent to Emily that she didn't have to help her if it made her feel too awkward, but Emily was stubborn. She drew a strange kind of power from the justice she felt in helping her mum. Emily didn't think she'd enjoy it as much as she did and even though it brought back memories of her dad (they both shed a tear or two) they bonded and set about their task of having a fresh start in their lives. At least a fresh start with all Wayne's stuff packed away in the garage anyway. So, Emily and Pam had a great time together, despite Wayne's exit and Emily's secret.

At times Emily wanted to burst out from the mind-blowing frustration of having to know about Eddie, Jack and 'Mom' and not being able to tell anyone (even her mother) but every time she was close to saying something (most likely to her mum) she managed to calm down and settle herself quietly.

"Don't be such a sissy Em!" she would scold herself. "No-one would listen to your story anyway! They'd think you're a nutter!"

If anything, her friendship with Eddie was now stronger, brought on by their shared experience. They did have some clumsy conversations in the days following Emily's epiphany and the unveiling of the true nature of her neighbours though. Mostly because Emily had to somehow get her head around the fact that whilst Eddie looked and talked (and acted convincingly) like a 10-year-old boy, he was in fact well over 400 years older than she was. This was no doubt weird and a bit creepy and even stranger for Eddie when you consider that he'd spent more time in his life just being a child.

You may laugh at such things, but Eddie did not. He didn't find that amusing at all.

"Hey freckle face!" Emily teased him "don't be such a........." Her banter was good for Eddie, however, as it wrested him from his melancholy and it was also good for Emily as it let her know that although Eddie was an incredibly old sorcerer, he could still be the normal, boring socially awkward boy you would meet on every school playground. With Eddie, Emily felt like an equal even though she knew darn well he was nothing like her. She didn't feel that he would ever 'talk down' to her like most grown-ups did and he certainly was not afraid of her questions. There was plenty of those too, but Eddie could not (or would not) answer all her questions. At times Emily would be resentful of his refusal to tell her something about their 'magic'.

"You might find out someday Em, but I cannot tell you myself" he would plead with her.

Emily tried to pester Eddie with dozens of questions and Eddie would do his best to accommodate her but there was some knowledge that was off limits and Emily would know by just looking into his eyes that he could not answer, and it was sincere.

That same week, whilst Eddie and Emily were exploring the woods above their street, two strangers appeared on the path next to Emily's house. No-one saw them.

They just. Arrived. No sound or wind. It was perhaps favourable that their presence didn't attract any attention at all because these two characters were quite strange. They looked out-of-place in the street of boring 1950's state houses. One of the strangers was very old and short, dressed in the clothes of a Hindu monk with a balding brown head and long wispy grey hairs sort of emanating from his skull in various directions. He held a stare of hunger, like he was supressing his internal ambition, but he was clearly quite chuffed with himself and his visage looked eager to do what he had come to do. The other stranger was tall and resembled an Elvish warrior. His hair was long and blond (superbly moisturised too) and he wore dark elegant leather garments with finely embroidered silver filigree along the hems. He gave the impression that he was a prince of high importance but was nevertheless ready to battle at a moment's notice. You couldn't see a weapon on him, but you instinctively knew that he would be carrying one regardless. His features were a mixture of a nasty scowl and a faraway look of intense sadness or mourning (or was it longing?). The older one spoke.

"The prophecy may yet be far from us, my friend. Much is yet to be learnt of the boy's significance", the Sharma said thoughtfully. His voice was old and quiet but rough like sandpaper, yet he held authority in his words too.

"Hmmmmm, much is closed off to me old man" Evantine murmured gravely. "I don't see that which you do. Not since the dark times has such uncertainty reigned supreme." Evantine fell silent, deep in his apparent troubles. He had the strong voice of a Nordic king; he voiced every word carefully and sincerely, meaning everything he said.

"It matters not right now, friend" Sharma comforted Evantine. Putting a hand on Evantine's great arms he faced him with his eager friendly smile.

"Let the boy explain" asked Sharma. "He has much to offer and is a great deal more powerful than he knows." Sharma chuckled knowingly to Evantine. The tall one grimaced at the monk's attempt at weak humour. There had been a few young 'members' over the centuries who had come unstuck. The hunting down and killing of the Nordic wizards and witches was only one example of how a local human population could become hysterical and murderous when a 'member' gets it wrong.

"That's my problem, old man" Evantine replied, constraining his indifference with force. "He doesn't know how much trouble he can cause!" He stopped. The old man was far too wise to respond to Evantine's provocation. The Nord swallowed his anguish instead and waited to follow the older man's lead.

They both stared up at the wood beyond the house (Eddie's), each pausing to consider something to himself and then with a nod to each other in mutual approval started walking towards the front door. They approached slowly but surely, like a slow-moving ferry coming into port, and had a menacing look to them, as if there were some troublesome tasks ahead and they didn't want to rush. Or perhaps it was because the old one was slowing the other down and in the process was frustrating the other's desire to resolve this quickly. Whatever the reason, it wouldn't matter. The 'tall one' didn't look like the sort you would mess with.

Mom had detected the arrival of the strange duo and went out to meet them as they walked up the steps.

"םכילע םולשו אבה ךורב" Mom babbled happily in her foreign tongue.

"aap par shaanti ho! hamaare mahaan eeshvar aapako aasheervaad de" Sharma replied enthusiastically. He was clearly happy to see her.

Jack descended the stairs to meet the guests. A serious look of foreboding couldn't be hidden from his face when he noticed Evantine had accompanied the Sharma.

"Welcome, honoured guests. Edward will be with us soon, masters" Jack spoke almost too politely at the two guests.

Evantine didn't seem to be concerned with Jack's displeasure at their arrival. If he was, he hid it well.

Pretending to smile graciously, Evantine chose his words carefully as he spoke to Jack. "Your generous hospitality is appreciated, Master Jack." The Nord did not wait for a reply but carried on as if not needing to follow social cues. "I know how much you care for him, but I must impose my will where it is of the utmost importance," Evantine asserted his dominance over Jack. "Edward will make his account and we will be... (he paused for dramatic effect) fair". Evantine continued his speech. "Much still is yet to be established and we know not of the dangers that lie ahead". He was irritatingly correct, but he was right about their lack of foresight into any dangers that could pose a threat to their mission. Jack knew only too well that the conditions would not suit either Jack or Mom, or even Eddie, but he dared not undermine a Master under any circumstances.

"Please, Masters" said Jack, attempting to diffuse some of the obvious tension. "You are most welcome in our house. Do come in."

"They come!" Mom declared, pointing up the hill. She was referring to Emily and Eddie who were a couple of dozen yards away, walking out of the woods above the house. It broke the tension sufficiently for Jack to avoid any possible conflicts with Evantine. Sharma appeared to be equally relieved and looked visibly eager to meet Emily.

They had timed their arrival with astonishing precision. Eddie and Emily had spent a few days just hanging out and so the exhilaration Emily had felt in the days after her discovery had waned quite significantly, leaving the possibility of her 'freaking out' at the two guests quite low. More so because Eddie, Jack and Mom had kept things as 'normal' as possible. She had almost begun to wonder whether it had all been just a crazy dream.

That would not ever be a problem again. There was no way possible that Eddie would be able to convince anyone that Sharma and Evantine were his 'uncles' either. They were so unusual that it would be absurd to even think it. Eddie tried to imagine himself saying:

"Hi, this is Evantine. He's a Finnish art dealer and his friend Sharma is a Hindu monk from Tibet". It was so impossibly preposterous there was no way he could say it with a straight face. At any rate, if Eddie did know about their arrival, he kept it from Emily and so her surprise at meeting them was utterly without pretence.

And so, a couple of days before Christmas in 1982, Sharma and Evantine would decide her fate and the result of their decision would reverberate for decades to come. The sheer monumental significance of Sharma and Evantine deciding Emily's destiny cannot be understated. There would be no arguing amongst the 'members'. If it was decided that her discovery of Eddie was of no great importance to the future of humanity or that of the council's policy, she would be one in a long line of people throughout the centuries who would simply be ignored and left to question their own sanity. One thing was for sure: those who were 'cut-off' from the members would never learn the truth of what and who they were. Ever.

Would they decide to let her continue as a child in the greatest knowledge mankind had ever known? If so, could she be trusted to not 'blow the cover' and would she be able to handle the immense pressure and stress that would come with it? Was it even the right thing to do?

To burden a child with such enormous responsibility wasn't just irresponsible, to some it was tantamount to madness.

However, when Emily met Sharma and Evantine, it was purely a delightful exchange of ideas and thoughts. At no time during their introduction would you have ever wondered if Emily was at all put off by their interest in her or even if she felt awkward at their strange appearance. In fact, the two Elders were fascinated by her sincere nature and Emily was a curious girl who asked the right questions.

"You are like Eddie, right?" she asked Sharma once the polite introductions were done. "But you are both much older than him and so much more important?" Emily blurted out a dozen questions in quick succession.

"Child, don't hurry yourself." said Sharma. "Yes, I am the oldest here, but I am not the wisest." His eyes glinted in mock humour at Emily.

"However, you must be warned," the old man said seriously now. "Many things you will learn tonight but many questions you will ask of us will go unanswered."

"It is no accident that you are here, my child." Sharma spoke quietly to Emily whilst the others listened patiently. "The Vision אמא (Mom) has shared with you is centuries old and has been kept secret to protect your life."

Emily's eyes widened in disbelief as what she heard was far beyond her imagination.

"Why me?" she asked, as the chilling reality of her situation dawned on her. "These things don't just happen to anyone, do they?" Emily was trying hard to grapple with her now tenuous hold on reality.

"Why me!" she repeated to the Sharma. Then, she remembered something chilling but equally significant to her. Her dream. It was a dream in which she saw a huge city being attacked by massive flying warships. The same dream in which someone wanted her to escape.

"It's my dream, isn't it?" Emily was looking at everyone now. For once in her life, elders were listening attentively to her questions with humble respect and thoughtfulness.

Eddie was finding it hard to constrain himself, standing there biting his lip nervously trying to supress his desire to answer Emily directly. He wouldn't though, besides, he had no knowledge of Emily's dream at all since she hadn't thought it was anything more than a silly dream. Instead, Eddie sat in silence. He would respect the elders right to answer her. Evantine was a blank face. He gave no impression of disdain for Emily neither did he even seem to be attentive to her questions. He merely said nothing and let Sharma lead the conversation. Jack and Mom were also quiet yet looked concerned when Sharma revealed the knowledge of the vision to Emily.

"Have they already decided?" thought Eddie suspiciously. Inwardly groaning to himself, he wondered why they would reveal such information to her already.

"Child, we know not of your dream or if it is even of any importance," the Sharma answered her. "We must ask the questions first and then decide our own fate."

"A great power far beyond your time and age has threatened annihilation many times over the centuries. Perhaps it is like the kind you saw in your dream?" He addressed Emily gravely.

Emily was stunned. They knew of her dream! How was that possible?

"You know my dream?!" she sounded almost hysterical now.

Then the Sharma did something quite strange. He went to Emily and knelt by her side. Not like a subject would kneel before a king, but like a parent comforting a child. Placing his old hand on her shoulder he spoke calmly and quietly.

Emily, not expecting the old man to be so warm and soothing, was calmed by his attention to her. He consoled her with a soft request.

"Child, with your permission we will share our visions with each other?"

Emily looked confused at his request. Share her vision? How is that possible? she thought. Mom noticed her bewilderment at Sharma's appeal and came to her side to help mitigate her fears.

Both Emily and Sharma nodded in approval of Mom's intervention. As per usual, Mom didn't hesitate. Mumbling again in her foreign language (words Emily only wished she could understand now more than ever) Mom projected a vision in front of them. It appeared like a hovering holographic image in front of Sharma, yet they could all see it.

They both looked at Emily in mute appeal. She knew what they were asking. They wanted her to try to remember the dream, but how would she be able to show them like the magic they performed in front of her?

She was no sorcerer! She was just an ordinary 10-year-old girl whose only skill was to play the piano. Emily needn't have worried. Without speaking, Evantine went to Emily and gently took her hand and placed it in his huge palm.

Then he uttered two words. "Syn Blitt". He spoke with authority and intensity then returned to where he'd been standing. Emily tried with great difficulty to recall her dream.

Suddenly, appearing before them were three identical visions of the same dream Emily had experienced months beforehand. Or should we say the dream was only 'sort of' identical. Emily stared with amazement at the three slightly different perspectives being displayed. Even Eddie who had seen many visions was almost overwhelmed by the sheer magnitude and detail of the dream. He let out a huge "Whoa!" when the dream came to its close. There, unmistakably, was Eddie appearing as a man in his late twenties telling Emily to 'go'.

He was as equally surprised and shocked as Emily. Never had he witnessed such an important conformity of visions. Mom had though. She was nodding to herself, and her eyes darted fearful looks at the Sharma, who nodded in a sad recognition of her concern. Sharma looked at Evantine. His old eyes, which had seen many centuries, now looked sad and his cheeky smile had been replaced by a sense of foreboding and doom. Evantine wasn't in a hurry to respond to the elder's mute distress, however, he was as staunch and unremitting in his self-control as always. Perhaps the Nordic was greatly more skilled in hiding his true emotions towards others, but, to Eddie's great surprise, he did offer words of encouragement to the group.

"It is no small thing, friends" Evantine spoke his words with strength and determination. "That we must offer the child protection is clear".

Eddie shot a glance of amazement at the Nord. Eddie wasn't expecting him to judge so early. His intentions were now laid bare for all to see. In one sentence, Evantine had proclaimed his stance and direction. "That we must offer the child protection" was repeating through Eddie's mind. Evantine had foregone the need to question the girl for hours and had made his decision without consulting Sharma. His sudden statement reverberated around the room as each person was taken aback by his forthright declaration and considered the ramifications of such an outcome. Evantine was now eager to find out how such a significant development was not mentioned to him earlier. The Sharma must have held the vision in his consciousness for decades or even centuries.

"How long have you suspected, old man?" the Nord questioned Sharma with a serious concern.

The old man shrugged as he answered his friend. "I only have small pieces of the puzzle, my friend. Only Edward was clear to me in the vision and neither the time or place made sense until 'אמא' could also confirm for me its importance".

"You know of this place?" Evantine asked.

"Somewhere in Southeast Urudesh perhaps? It is hard to tell as the buildings and vehicles are much more advanced than now." Sharma went on to explain. "For decades, centuries even, I have considered dozens of these 'visions' and many are still a mystery to me".

"It is foolish to run after every rabbit the runs into a hole. Better to wait and catch one when they come back out". The Sharma winked. "If you have the patience of course". He grinned.

Evantine held his stare for a few seconds as the room went silent. All eyes were on Evantine now.

"You are much wiser than you confess, old man". Evantine said gesturing with a sincere smile to Sharma. "Much wiser than I. It was risky and perhaps dangerous not to share such important knowledge with the rest of us, but I see now that you have made an enlightened choice, my friend!"

Evantine was right. The wrong knowledge of the smallish details of future events could have grave consequences for millions of people.

Even worse if that information fell into the hands of those willing to harness such power for selfish means. That would be devastating. Everyone in the room was thinking a similar thing.

“Does that mean the vision confirms our deepest fears?” wondered Eddie. He dared not speak his thoughts aloud right now. It was clear that a deep foreboding hovered over the small company. Apprehension now clearly visible on Jack’s brow as he grasped the magnitude of the Nord’s wishes. Everyone seemed to be waiting for a statement from either Evantine or Sharma. Neither appeared in any hurry to calm Eddie’s great discomfort. Emily was also attentive to the subtle social queues and felt the worry and tension in the room, so she decided to remain quiet too. She shot a look of mute appeal to Eddie, but he was unable to return her request as the Sharma had broken the tense silence.

“We are not helpless my friends!” Sharma spoke to the group. Smiling at Emily who was struggling to comprehend everything that had taken place. She didn’t understand the things that Evantine spoke of, and they were speaking of her dream like it was a real place and a REAL event in the future. She was becoming scared now, her previous confidence and safety had disappeared.

Her thoughts were getting muddled, and her head was swimming with the ideas of danger. She was just a kid! What was all this talk about centuries old prophecies and some place in Urudesh! Why should she care? Was this some sort of cruel hoax or some game that these new neighbours liked to play?

Emily wasn’t handling this at all well. Very soon she would be hysterical and that wouldn’t bode well for her or the group. Jack had already noticed that Emily was struggling to understand what was happening and he rose to assist her.

“Emily is not coping. I must return her to her mother,” he spoke with such authority that no one, not even Evantine, attempted to block him from taking Emily. He put his arm around her and stood her up.

Emily, needing the attention and care, went with him without question. His strong, sure, grip was comforting and eased her distress. She really did need a good distraction from the seriousness of the day's events. Jack walked Emily home as the others discussed the vision's augury. As always, Jack was a superb communicator and returned the distraught Emily home (across the street) to her mum, who was busy preparing a meal for the guests she was expecting later that day.

"Are you ok, Bun?" Pamela asked Emily.

"I just got... a little scared I guess," she lied terribly. "There's strange noises up in the woods you know Mum." Emily tried to cover for Jack. If Jack noticed, he didn't show it and Pamela certainly didn't seem overly concerned either. Kids were always running around in the woods, playing and inventing. There was really no reason for Pamela to suspect anything overtly sinister about Emily's turmoil. Emily needn't have tried making up a cover story for Jack as he was quite capable of handling the situation. He had discerned that Emily needed to get away from the serious nature of where Evantine might have been leading the 'meeting'. It was a wise move, to shield Emily from the pressure and magnitude of the augury, and what it could mean to her. Emily was grateful to Jack for helping as she (for once) was having trouble mouthing her distress to her companions let alone comprehending her part in the vision.

"I'm fine, Mum! I'm just gonna go and lie down and read for a while" she lied.

"Ok, Bun" replied Pam, "but you're coming with me to pick up Uncle Bob and Mary from the train station later, alright?"

Pamela winked, "Kids, eh?" she rolled her eyes at Jack. He didn't attempt to return her socially awkward gesture and turned to leave. As he did, however, Emily rushed forward and gave him a gentle hug. "Thanks for bringing me home, Mr Jack," she whispered "and don't worry, I won't tell your secret". Jack returned her hug and left Pamela and Emily on their doorstep. Pamela was now gazing in wonder at her daughter's affection for their new neighbour.

"Wow, you must've really got a fright eh, Bun?" she remarked, but Emily was already walking to her bedroom. As she sat there listening to her Bill Collins cassette tape (her dad had left it), the song "I've Been Waiting" had a haunting effect on her and it made her wonder at the vision she had witnessed. She'd experienced a terrible sense of danger, like the singer in the song It was scary and exceptionally weird.

Emily didn't have time to spend reflecting on her dream because her mum soon called her to go and collect her uncle and Aunt. It would be a perfect interruption for her thoughts. Uncle Bob loved to play the piano loudly and Emily knew that when they returned from the train station there would be lots of laughter and loud singing of pop songs and carols into the night. Emily chose to put it out of her mind as there would be plenty of time later for worry and distress over the future. She managed this quite well, I might add. The next few days were a harmony of good spirits, family jokes and great food for the Christmas break.

When Jack returned to their house, Evantine and Sharma had finished questioning Eddie and were relaying to him the importance of his 'new mission'. Eddie didn't seem very happy with whatever Evantine had instructed and it wasn't just Eddie's lack of enthusiasm either. Eddie seemed to dislike Evantine immensely, or was it mistrust? Evantine equally seemed to treat Eddie with little regard and didn't try hard to hide his disdain for Eddie. Was it because Eddie was a boy that Evantine disregarded him so callously? Was it because the Nord was an elder that Eddie was uncomfortable taking directions from someone apparently so removed from their predicament? Whatever the reason, the tension was almost palpable, and you could hear in Eddie's voice that he was constraining his anger well. Evantine held his self-control in check also and did well to not provoke the younger member. Eddie was arguing his case with the elders when Jack returned.

"I must know the depth of the danger if I'm to protect her indefinitely!" he addressed them both. "To blindly follow your 'orders' without an explanation is unacceptable to me!"

"Eddie!" Evantine scowled at the young man. "There are greater dangers and risks that threaten our mission. Not just you! You must put aside this petty setback and help us." Evantine was doing well to reason with Eddie.

Evantine had 'ordered' Eddie to shadow Emily indefinitely and that was no small thing to consider even for someone as old as Eddie. His 'protection' of Emily could span decades of faithful service to the cause. Evantine had unfairly added a clause to his protection detail, one which Eddie despised. He insisted that Eddie not actively seek out possible threats against Emily as it could lead to her being threatened earlier. And when one goes looking for trouble, it doesn't usually take a person long to find some. Eddie would be a magnet for trouble. His hunger for justice and his care for Emily could prove too dangerous for them both. So Evantine had instructed him to be as passive as possible and to leave the discreet investigation of dangers to them. Eddie was visibly unhappy but eventually he was persuaded to agree to the conditions.

"If the enemy discovers you, then they will discover Emily and we cannot risk such dangers." Sharma now interceded for Evantine, trying to appeal to Eddie's sense of reason.

"Okay, Okay, OKAAAAY!" Eddie settled it in frustration. He paused and gathered his thoughts, settling his nerves before speaking to the elders. "I will do it, for her," he said, then added "and may G'd watch our paths with favour". He ended his declaration with a formal bow to both Elders and a sigh of relief was heard coming from Mom who had (like Jack) stayed quiet for most of the proceedings.

The elders may have set unfair conditions on him, but deep-down Eddie, Jack and Mom knew that it was the wisest option and Sharma had proven himself to be incredibly wise. Eddie had, for an exceptionally long time, trusted the old man, so his commitment to Emily would be sincere. Sharma was also special to Eddie as he had learned under Sharma more than four centuries ago when he was just developing his skill as a master shapeshifter. Sharma was more than just an 'elder' to Eddie. He had patiently and gently coached the young member's special abilities. At first, Eddie had been extremely frustrated and unable to jump more than a dozen yards, yet he had shown an early, natural skill for shapeshifting which had impressed the old man. Even back then, the Sharma noticed Eddie's resentment towards his skill. Eddie had loathed his inability to shapeshift beyond a man in his twenties. "Like so many young people," thought the elder, "so eager to desire what others have and yet unable to value their own expertise".

"You are special to me, and special to our brethren," Sharma spoke to Eddie. "Our bonds of service extend far beyond that of the Adami." His voice was low and sincere, and his expression emanated his raw, heartfelt care for Eddie. Addressing Jack and Mom, he spoke louder and with more authority.

"We will not fail you, brothers and sister."

"meree shaanti main tumhaare saath chhod deta hoon. bhagavaan aapakee raksha kare kyonki vah meree raksha karata hai" Sharma was ending his congress with a formal prayer.

They all understood, except Evantine who was not so greatly skilled in language. He didn't need to know the exact translation anyway. He addressed Eddie first. With a deep frown, that could've been mistaken for indignation, he spoke slowly, and his words seemed to contradict his expression.

"Our strength goes ahead of you, young one. I will watch over you as will our brethren". The Nord addressed Eddie formally, yet he found it difficult to accept his kind words of encouragement.

Eddie nodded his mute approval to the Nordic elder and Evantine, then directed his formal goodbye to Jack and Mom before leaving with Sharma. In a few moments the house was quiet and the three sat there each in their own deep contemplation. For a while, all that could be heard was the wind rustling through the trees outside, inside the occasional crackle of wood burning in the hearth and neither was there any movement but for a flicker of a candle. Eddie was stunned by how quickly their whole world had changed from a boring 'arse-end-of-the-world' surveillance mission to a decades-long commitment which could determine the outcome for possibly millions of people from annihilation at some time in the future.

Eddie thought about Emily and how unprepared she was for this world. She didn't know anything of the grave horrors he had encountered in the many wars he had witnessed. The sheer extent of this violence had shaken Eddie and it had taken him decades to recover from the trauma. He realised now that his time in El Anil (LINQ) had been very therapeutic and had rejuvenated his soul. Still, Eddie half wished that Emily could be spared from having to cope with a terrible prophecy hanging over her future. He thought it unfair that she understood extraordinarily little about these dangers, but he knew she would not have to face them alone. Eddie had made a solemn vow to the elders and to Emily. He would not break that vow. Ever.

Meanwhile on the other side of town.

There was a loud crash. The door had easily broken from Brian smashing the full force of his weight into it. You see, Brian was robbing the local dairy because he'd run out of cigarettes, and he knew that the dairy owner just happened to be away that night. Having had the brilliant fortune of overhearing the owner speaking to an elderly lady in the shop a few days earlier, whilst Brian was surreptitiously trying to thieve some magazines, the owner had let slip he'd be away. "But only for a night mind you!" he stated "don't want none of the lads going without the morning paper now do we?!" Brian was lucky the owner was away that night because had the owner discovered Brian stealing from his shop, the young lad might've finished his sad evening in the hospital (or worse). Luckily for Brian (or unluckily), a young policeman (Matt) was doing his patrol in the area and detected the sound of the door breaking a few houses away from the tiny shopping centre.

Brian, totally oblivious to his silent pursuer, grabbed at cigarette packets and papers and chuckled to himself "and a few of these here nice, wee gobstoppers for the road eh," whilst filling his pockets with sweets from behind the counter.

"Ahem!" coughed Matt loudly, standing on the broken doorway and blocking the exit.

"Don't bother running Brian, there's a copper out the back so ya needn't break that door too, right?" Matt lied spectacularly, eyeing up the back door as he spoke.

Brian was fooled. Brian was a career fool though. Sharing a dirty, mouldy flat with some equally morally irresponsible young men was Brian's way of asserting his misguided dominance over society. His unwillingness to work was his 'political' activism coupled with not being a 'namby pamby' to those elitist corporate twats. Brian was quite happy to take his share of financial benefits from the government though. Taking the government's money was an act of defiance and in his mind, it was 'showing those tossers'. The money that he did receive was never enough, however, and the power almost certainly got cut off every other month when he'd have to sucker up to his parents for a loan. Leather boots weren't cheap and black trench coats and hair gel didn't come for free. You had to steal them otherwise you'd have to pay for them, right? And 'paying' for things went against his 'political' right to be a self-righteous freeloading git.

Brian had a brilliant logic to life that only he and his comrades could understand. As career options went, Brian was now looking at having a short holiday behind bars, at least for a couple of nights until the Courts opened on Monday morning. "Two days without a cigarette!" whined Brian when he realised his ill fortune.

"Count yourself lucky!" Matt scoffed at Brian in amusement. "If Slattery had been there, you might not have had any lips left to smoke with!" Matt laughed loudly to himself. He never could understand how idiots like Brian even made it past high school without doing some grave, irreparable harm to their brains through being such idiots.

Matt Ferguson was a brilliant cop. The thing that people liked about him was his friendly nature. Sometimes the local coppers tended to be a bit over-the-top and authoritarian. A few of Matt's colleagues had been given the word by their captain to mind their fists on the beat. The 'beat' was when two officers would walk a neighbourhood for a few hours, looking out for trouble and we all know that trouble isn't usually too hard to find when you're a young 'action-hungry' violence-prone police officer. The local councils liked the cops to be out-and-about where people could see them. That way they'd 'put off' anyone having a good think about doing something stupid. More often than not, someone was always thinking about doing something stupid and Matt had a natural instinct for finding them. The trouble for the coppers wasn't only the cons they were chasing day and night and sometimes it wasn't even the 'beat' that was the problem for the officers either. Too often the wives of the officers ended up bearing the brunt of the policeman's failure to deal with his frustration on the job. Matt wasn't like those cops, and he wasn't young and naive which some would like to imagine. On many occasions, when faced with abusive and violent behaviour, Matt's ability to 'talk' a nutter down proved more helpful and saved the knuckles of a few of the officers he was with.

So, what was Matt's problem? Well, he cared. He cared about people and that sort of thing was bound to get in the way of doing your job when you're having to 'put up' with idiots like Brian every second night. Still, as Matt drove Brian (cuffed) to the station for processing, he appealed to Brian and asked him what sort of life he expected to get from stealing smokes. Matt would pressure cons to think about the stupid things they did. On some occasions it was an ingenious tactic because the guy (or girl) would end up spilling the beans on something else stupid they'd done and end up getting charged for both. Matt might've cared but he was a sharp officer and everyone who knew him, knew it too.

This evening in the station, Matt was trying to be friendly to Brian and reason with him while he processed the case. Matt's stubbornness to keep questioning Brian was personal as well.

"Come on Brian" Matt pleaded, "I know your mom and she'll be worried about ya you know? Don't you know my uncle runs a shift at Donaghy's? I can get you a few hours if ya promise to sort yourself out?"

Matt's attention to his prisoner had caught the eye of one of the detectives standing nearby. "You are wastin' your time Matty!" he scorned. "This punk will just be back for more." Coming in close to Brian's face, the senior detective liked intimidating the young hoodlums that got brought into the station. "We've just got a fresh shipment of new phonebooks too". He pointed to the new stacks. "They're a bit bigger than last year and I'll betcha that won't tickle eh boy!?!" Detective Lewis cackled hysterically trying to scare the boy as much as possible. Phonebooks were an effective tool for beating prisoners (or so they thought). The idea was simple, using a big heavy phonebook to hit prisoners within their cells was supposed to leave less bruising and inflict maximum pain, however this didn't consider the honest folk like Matt who fought to stop such violent behaviour in the cells.

Matt grimaced and tried to hide his embarrassment at the detective's foul display of superiority. But neither Brian or Lewis had any care for what Matt thought about them; they both were equally narcissistic and were too busy focusing on their own schemes. There were far worse places to be than the cells at the central police station. Prison wardens were generally a good bunch and usually separated out the violent prisoners from the young ones like Brian. For much of his lonely weekend in the cells, he went without his cigarettes and avoided any 'beatings' from overly enthusiastic prisoners looking for someone to intimidate.

On Monday, when Matt came to deliver Brian to the courts, he came bearing news that Brian's fortune had changed.

"Slattery wouldn't lay charges against you so you're free to go," Matt lied. He could've laid charges against the lad himself, but he wanted to give the boy a chance. Brian's mum had pleaded with Slattery to let them repair the damage to the shop and begged him not to press charges. Strangely the grumpy, old dairy owner agreed. It was a small town and even Matt's parents knew the Slattery's well enough.

Brian's fortune wasn't all wine and roses though. As Matt led Brian out to the station car park, Detective Lewis spotted the duo and went straight for them. Rushing forward without any regard for his colleague, Lewis grabbed at the boy's hooded top roughly and pushed him hard against the vehicle.

"Lettin' 'em get away eh". Lewis sneered at Matt whilst holding Brian as hard as he could. Lewis was a tall chap, much older than Matt, and had big hands and a rough looking bushy moustache. He liked intimidating people and drew great pleasure from threatening young punks like Brian to see whether they would crack.

"Should've locked 'im up and sent 'im to the judge. You're a fool, Ferguson!" Lewis spat his words at the younger policeman. Matt chose not to respond to the angry detective. He'd seen this performance a few times now.

Lewis pushed Matt out of his way and grabbed Brian. It was an easy thing for a tall man like Lewis as Brian was a wiry, young man. It almost looked like a father about to beat a child from the right perspective. Lewis was fully intending to get the most out of it while he had the time. Matt, on the other hand, was unlikely to let Lewis intimidate a freed prisoner for much longer and was sure that stuck-up Ferguson would report him if he injured the young lad.

"I overheard a young friend of yours telling some old boys down the pub a few weeks ago, bragging about someone who'd been stealing some of Farmer John's chickens. He sounded a lot like your scum......."

Lewis eyed the boy testily to see if the bait had any effect. Unfortunately, Brian was either too scared to react or far too good at pretending not to care, but either way he gave Lewis nothing. Lewis was seething with rage and his face was now turning a deep crimson. He knew he had nothing though and would have to leave it for now, so he released his grip.

"If I catch you boy!" Lewis threatened. "Don't think you'll get any of that namby-pamby treatment you got from your good mate here! I'll give you a good thrashing myself if I see ya again".

"Don't waste your time with these losers, Matt!" Lewis rasped angrily. "Pretty soon the Royals will be 'ere and you'll 'ave plenty of idiots to clear outta the city". Lewis, regaining his composure, adjusted his suit jacket and hat before stomping away from the duo.

Brian was shaken and was trembling a bit, but he wasn't stupid. He'd heard what Lewis had said and locked it away for later.

"The Royals are coming to Dooners!" He thought excitedly. "Oh, that's good, that's verrrrry good". Brian was already scheming something as equally stupid as the dairy robbery. Hiding his unexpected good fortune, Brian tried to keep a scared look on his face and failed miserably because Brian was a class idiot. He ended up smirking like a child holding a lollipop.

"Well," said Matt trying to defuse the tension, "that could've gone worse!" Matt must've been expecting Lewis to punch the kid and 'teach' him a lesson. He was relieved. He didn't need that on his conscience as he'd probably have to explain it to Brian's mum and dad later, not to mention that reporting a fellow colleague for misconduct was virtually non-existent in the force. Lewis was being an enormous bowl of ass and Matt would probably have to cover for him.

Matt got Brian into the car while he regained his thoughts. What Lewis had said about the chickens was interesting. It was like Lewis was quoting Farmer John word for word. Matt guessed that Lewis had just been trying to bait Brian in case he got lucky, so Matt decided to try his own and maybe joke about it instead. "Who knows?" considered Matt, "maybe he'll spill the beans to me!"

"You been hanging 'round Farmer John's, Brian?" Matt tried not to laugh.

"Piss off!" Brian replied. He liked Constable Matt, but he knew better than to tell him anything.

As Matt drove Brian home, he tried again to reason with him, but Brian was miles away, daydreaming about what he could get up to while all the officers were busy doing 'security' for the royal visit. Brian may have been an idiot, but he was a very clever idiot. He knew that while the police were preoccupied, he'd probably be able to skim a few shops and even get away with it. Next time he'd be more careful.

CHAPTER 04
FRIENDS AND FOE

A few weeks had passed since Sharma and Evantine met Emily and then left to attend to their secret pursuits. It was nearing the end of the summer break for Emily and the Christmas holidays had been a welcome distraction from her weird encounter with the elders. Truth be told, she would've been happy to forget that it had happened altogether and move on with her boring life, without the fearful warnings of a future with great warships and thousands of innocent people dying. Emily was still having trouble trying to forget her strange dream.

Ignoring Eddie had been the hardest thing she had ever done though. She considered Eddie probably the closest friend she had, yet in the week after Christmas, when all the excitement had died down and her extended family had departed, she resisted the urge to see him. And she had a weak excuse to use. Her mum wasn't going back to work for a couple of weeks, so it became an easy justification to ignore Eddie and avoid having to deal with the seriousness and frightening results of the vision she had witnessed. When her mum asked if she was gonna go play with Eddie on this day or that, she could make up any excuse not to go over there.

"Nah mum, I just wanna go with you today" Emily would say, or "I'm just gonna read my books today cos Eddie is busy," she would lie.

Pamela was wise enough not to question Emily too much on her reasons for avoiding her best friend. Children can be fickle with friendships, especially 10-year-old girls. Pamela wouldn't want to intervene and make things worse by trying to 'rescue' something that wasn't any of her business. Emily only had so many excuses not to talk with Eddie, however, and sooner rather than later they would both have to go back to school. She only hoped that things could return to normal, and all the weird stuff was just a crazy hoax. It wasn't that Emily was angry at Eddie. Not at all. She sometimes felt intense remorse for ignoring her friend and wondered if that was what her dad felt, if he ever stopped and considered his feelings about things. Emily didn't really want to wonder about her dad though. That was another hurtful memory she'd rather forget too.

Eddie had decided to not 'push' it with Emily. Besides, it wasn't in his nature to be assertive and pushy. He was more of a passive personality who was very comfortable in his own company anyway. By the second week of January, however, both Jack and Mom had started to bring the subject up with Eddie.

"How's Emily today?" Jack would subtly ask Eddie. "Is everything alright do you think?"

"Isz Emeely hhccommeeeeng today, Eeedee?" Mom would prod him playfully, hoping for a response from him.

But Eddie wasn't keen on being too assertive and risk pushing Emily away even further so was happy to keep his distance. One day, after consulting quietly with Mom, Jack decided to try a diplomatic approach with Eddie to see whether he could achieve at least something better than nothing.

"I've got an idea Ed," said Jack. "There's a lake district a couple of hundred miles south of here that you would love. I think a holiday would be good for us, yes?"

"You know we can't leave Emily," said Eddie. "Isn't that a bit risky?" he added. Jack as per usual was four steps ahead of Eddie.

"Maybe we can invite Pamela and Emily to come away with us for a few days?" Jack asked cunningly.

Eddie loved exploring but, since the elders had left, they had stayed as close to Emily as possible (now that they couldn't risk leaving her in any chance of danger). He was always keen to get 'out-and-about' and discover new places. Jack said the southern lakes wouldn't disappoint and, at this time of year, it would be the hottest place in the country but surprisingly hardly anyone would be around. That wasn't exactly true but compared to El Anil it was virtually a ghost town. "Jack, do you really think you can convince Pam to drop her plans and travel hundreds of miles on a spontaneous adventure?" asked Eddie.

"Not sure," replied Jack. "But I'll bet they can't say no when we pay for it," Jack suggested. Eddie had little knowledge of their finances as Mom and Jack tended to the more 'boring' jobs such as maintenance and money. Nevertheless, he wasn't surprised at Jack's ability to gather the necessary 'rescurces' he needed for a mission. Usually, their missions required them to be almost invisible, so they tended to use very humble belongings to mask their true nature. It was a bold move that Jack had suggested, but it was also a good one.

Eddie laughed. For probably the first time in days his mood lifted, and he saw the genius of Jack's idea.

"Ok," replied Eddie. "But I think you should be the one who asks, since it's your great idea".

Jack gave him a look of feigned reproach. "What? Me do all the hard work too?!" then he jovially gave Eddie a seriously fatherly look. "Can't have you upsetting the girls now, can we young man!" He punched Eddie's arm playfully hoping to antagonise him more, Eddie's face breaking into a coy smile to mock him back.

Jack's plan worked and his offer was accepted by Pamela, although Emily didn't exactly sound too positive when Jack overheard Pamela telling her about their unexpected holiday. Next week, they would stay in one of the old civil works houses that Jack had arranged to rent for the week. It wasn't, by any standard, a luxury accommodation, but neither Emily nor Pam would care too much, and Jack had a knack for finding bargains. In fact, he had already managed to hire a good-sized motorboat and a vehicle to pull it.

"Come," Jack beckoned to Eddie, "I have something to show you". With a look of curiosity, Eddie followed Jack downstairs, underneath the house. When they'd arrived months ago, they had transformed the building's upper floors but because there was no garage or vehicle driveway access to any of the old state houses on the street, Jack had decided he would develop his own bunker under the house.

Eddie had taken very little notice of Jack's work so when he descended the stairs his awe was visible. Like the 'magic' that they had conjured to transform the house above, the basement had been spectacularly altered to resemble a huge workshop. It was transfigured so accurately that even its massively high ceiling resembled a warehouse with 'natural' light coming in through semi-transparent roofing. There were work benches, tables, various toolboxes, and huge locked cupboards lining the 'walls'. The whole place was like a modern-day factory. It was exceptionally clean, and one corner looked just like a sterile laboratory. In the centre was a dais of about 2 metres across, big enough for three or four people to stand on comfortably.

"Whoa!" exclaimed Eddie. "You've been busy, haven't you?" Eddie was confused though. "Why do we need all this? What if this gets discovered too?"

"It won't," replied Jack. "It can't be. I doubt even the Nord would notice anything more than a wine cellar down here, if he cared to look." He shot a look of satisfaction towards the boy.

"Mom and I have been working for decades on extremely old spells. Even before Sharma's time there was great need for 'subtlety'." He winked at Eddie. "This is a powerful spell Ed; it protects us from the greatest dangers and cannot be found by any person except us."

Eddie let out a long whistle of astonishment. He pointed to the dais. "Is that what you mean?" It didn't look like anything of great importance at all, just a circle of roughly plastered and poorly painted clay that rose about 30cm off the workshop floor. There were no visible signs that it held any significance other than it was situated in the centre of the room. It looked extremely old, almost primitive, as if made by hands or ancient hand tools.

"Yes," Jack answered. "The dais is our sanctuary, but it is also our transport." He gestured to a map on one of the tables next to him. It was of the Anderson Islands. A large circle was drawn in red, centred around the city of Doon, and extended to the equivalent of about 200 miles from the middle to its furthest point. Eddie was startled at the distance the circle represented.

"You mean we can jump anywhere in this circle?" Eddie asked incredulously. "I can barely jump 10 miles by myself. Are you sure this works?" he questioned.

Jack laughed loudly. "Yes Ed, from anywhere in that circle you can safely jump back here. However, you must never bring anyone with you under any circumstances."

Eddie eyes narrowed. "Not even to save Emily?" he asked.

"I don't know," Jack replied earnestly. "It could break a person's mind to return here with a stranger. You see, the jump only protects the house's occupants, and the spell could very well try to protect the house from any intruders. Even Emily!" he explained. No doubt he was being genuine in his warnings, but Eddie was sceptical and wanted to press Jack for more answers. Jack could see the worry in Eddie's eyes and tried to allay his fears as best he could.

"I haven't tried yet and truthfully I don't know if I want to consider it either," Jack faced him soberly. "Take my hand and I will show you."

Jack stood on the dais and Eddie grabbed his arm. In one sweeping motion both were instantly transported to a hillside farm many miles from the city. They stood in an old derelict single room house that had been destroyed many decades before. The fireplace was still largely intact, but the house's structure was mostly gone, and parts of the ring foundation were broken or had fallen over many years before. They both stood on what was left of the concrete slab which stopped the fireplace from falling over. It wasn't big and it wasn't pretty, but Eddie could see the logic in choosing such a place. It was a very remote location and obviously the farmer who owned the land had no desire to finish demolishing the old house either. Jack crawled into the dirty broken fireplace and beckoned Eddie to follow. They were instantly transported to a small cave that had been finely transformed into a temporary habitat for a few people. It was about the same size as a small cottage and the walls were lit with what appeared to be candle-like objects. They stood now on a much smaller dais in the cave. Here, Jack explained further. "This is as secure as our house and this dais links to the others also. You saw the entrance? We'll go back out that way." Jack wasn't interested in hanging around and catching a glimpse of Eddie's fascination and curiosity.

"We must keep moving!" Jack instructed the boy. Looking hurried, he held out his arm again to Eddie and they returned to the old fireplace. Jack felt that Eddie deserved a decent explanation now.

"I have four of these for us already and more planned," Jack instructed, "but it takes time and effort to make the links and secure them".

"How long?" asked Eddie.

"Hard to say Ed, I don't know what sort of dangers we may yet face". A look of serious determination set on Jack's face. "I can tell you that neither Sharma or Evantine know about these secure portals," he added. "And I'd rather they didn't either; the less they know the better".

"Wow," thought Eddie. "Even Jack doesn't trust the Nord?!" he shook his head in incredulity at Jack's wisdom. Jack walked off into one of the paddocks a way down the hill and returned a few minutes later carrying a small lamb in his arms. "Let's test your theory, Ed" he said, offering his outstretched arm. Eddie grabbed Jack's arm again and they returned safely to the dais in their secure bunker underneath the house. The lamb had been reduced to ashes and the dust fell to the cold dais at their feet.

"Wow!" Eddie shouted in surprise at the lamb's sudden immolation. "I had no idea, Jack!"

"Who knows if Emily would survive if you brought her back here, Ed" said Jack gravely. "Until we can be sure, you must not risk anything". He looked at Eddie, waiting for an answer.

"Ed, you must promise to not bring anyone here. I must have your word". Jack pressed Eddie for his oath.

"Of course, Jack". Eddie replied sincerely. "You have my word."

They ascended the stairs back up to the house and were met by Mom. She looked uneasy and ruffled. Sharma was waiting for them in the living room. He greeted them as kindly as he always did but seemed anxious to explain his unscheduled visit.

"My apologies friends, but Prince Dowling has requested a secret meeting with 'Us' when he arrives in late April." He spoke to them both. "That King Melville cannot travel himself is problematic and he has entrusted Dowling with this grave diplomatic mission".

The Sharma looked deeply concerned at the gravity of the request made by the monarch. Long ago, before Melville was King of Moray, Eddie had been placed in the service of protecting the future monarch. He was only 8 years old at the time, political upheaval was the norm and Waldron (a very old Cheseldek nation) was beginning once again to flex its muscles on the great continent. Various sources about the sprawling Moray Empire were gathering vital information that could assist in the monumental task of having to protect oneself from the horrifying possibility of an attack from Waldron. Another 'Member' had confirmed a vision like Emily's that showed the future monarch being put in danger and had convinced the Sharma to place the prince under the most extreme protection conditions possible. Since Eddie had such skill at shapeshifting, he was entrusted to the security detail. The pair had become close buddies, their friendship lasting for decades and earning the Council complete guarantees of secrecy from the royal family. That trust had not been possible amongst the kings and queens of Europe for a long time, and it had earned Eddie the respect of his kin. Jack and 'Mom' were assigned to him as modest protection too and to ensure his role went undetected by anyone who was curious enough to look.

The King obviously trusted his son with much more than just touring the Antipodes on a 'meet-and-greet' mission to the colonies. The prince had unquestionably earned the trust of the monarch with some of the Empire's greatest secrets and vulnerabilities. Eddie had met the young prince on a few occasions and was greatly impressed by his sincere, caring nature. Like his father, he wasn't complacent about his responsibility to ensure the ongoing safety and wellbeing of the Empire. Was it likely that the royal tour was just a 'cover' so that the prince could steal a secret meeting with the Council? It wouldn't be the first time that the Royals had had to plan for months just to get a few minutes alone with one of the members. Disclosure was taken as seriously by the members themselves as by the King. So how many people knew about the Council? If the King was to be trusted, then not even his son would know the entire truth. He would likely be told that a super-secret group of intelligence officers were commissioned by the crown to undertake certain 'missions' on his behalf. The Sharma would most likely know if a person disclosed knowledge of a member to anyone and besides, as far as Eddie was concerned, the King was to be trusted. Sharma knew that and Jack knew it too. He could trust the King with his life.

"It must be of great importance if the King has authorised the Prince to carry out his bidding." the Sharma told them. "I will accept the King's request and instruct his royal guard to arrange the meeting, but I must tell you now, we have considerable dangers to keep in mind."

"I presume the royal visit is to take place just before the school holidays in late April, yes?" asked Eddie contemplating the timing severely. "The difficulty of watching Emily and meeting the Prince can't be understated, surely?"

The Sharma considered Eddie with a look of grave concern. Eddie was right. Trying to bite off too much was always a recipe for disaster for any member. There was only so much that could be done, and it was still impossible to be in two places at one time.

"I have given your predicament due consideration and Evantine and myself will assist in the security of you both, as will Jack and 'אמא' (Mom)." the Sharma replied.

"It has not been since the Nina conflict that our friends have reached out to us!" Jack interjected. "Surely the King's need is far greater than a little girl!"

"Yes, and no" replied the Sharma. "There have been four decades of peace now and the threat has largely been contained. We must trust that Emily's future is just as important as the King's."

Jack looked confused by the Sharma's surprising answer to his question. "Emily is more important than the King?" he wondered. Still, they had months to prepare, and Eddie was more than capable of 'handling' himself. Jack would have to find a way to construct a 'safe' room for the Prince to conduct his business to ensure the King's message was conveyed privately and was already concentrating on ways to plan this when Sharma abruptly announced he was leaving.

"I must go," declared the Sharma, "and you must watch the girl at all costs." With that, he disappeared.

The next day, the two unusual families set out on their journey to the lakes. After some awkward encounters between Eddie and Emily, they all crammed into the hired sedan and were off. Emily hadn't wanted to be reminded of her strange encounter with magic, so seeing Eddie, Jack and Mom again was difficult at first. However, her anxiety was all but diffused by a friendly grin from Jack and a big hug from matronly Mom. Emily did her best to be as stand-offish as possible with Eddie and the cramped drive was no exception to that. It was a long way and the car had atrocious suspension. Eddie's back was sore from the long journey and the vinyl seats burned in the summer heat, not to mention the metal seat belt clasps that scorched your skin if the sun had been on them for a while. The drive to the lakes was not as bad as it could've been though, with most of the windows wound down to cool the vehicle as they drove, they spent their time shouting at each other over the sound of the wind and the road. Pamela taught them silly driving songs and games like 'B.I.N.G.O.' and 'eye-spy' and even Emily had been amused at hearing Mom's accent trying to sing the words.

Their excitement was palpable as the clear skies met them in the huge valley of the lakes. The town nearby was just a small village and it had one shop that serviced everything for the tiny population who lived there. Quite a few holiday makers were there from around the lakes where they camped in various sites, so it was unnaturally busy that day. The town was in the middle of a wide valley with towering mountains either side. The valley was a beautiful flat tundra of long dry grasses and lavender lining the paddocks and roads that covered the valley floor. It was hot but a light breeze fluttered down the length of the valley somewhat easing their discomfort from the stifling heat.

Pamela suggested that the group should all enjoy a national treasure: Trumpet ice creams. Emily's face lit up like a Christmas tree.

"Oh yes Mum!" she exclaimed. "That's the perfect idea after that rotten journey!" It really hadn't been all that bad, but no-one turns down a Trumpet ice cream on a hot day in summer.

So, the travellers all lined up at the busy village store. As they departed the store with their cold treats, Emily let out a disappointed sigh.

"Ugh! You wouldn't believe it!" she burst in apparent frustration. "Why does HE have to be here!" Emily was pointing to Brent (the bully in her class at school) who up until that point hadn't noticed their familiar group of travellers. Brent was with his parents and some cousins. They had obviously stopped at the shop for the same reason and when Brent noticed the pair, his face broke into a false grin. He decided to try his luck at a bit of fun. As he approached, he yelled out. "Not here with that loser are ya?" he taunted, fixing his attention on Emily, and then, having spotted the old sedan they'd obviously travelled in, he couldn't help but mock them.

"You made it here in that piece of junk?!" Brent pointed to their car in disgust. He was aiming to inflict as much verbal damage as possible whilst his parents were ignoring him.

Fortunately for Brent his father called him back, robbing Emily of a chance to humiliate him in return. "I hope you're staying close to us," Brent taunted Emily as he walked away, "I could use some target practice." He laughed cynically whilst pretending to shoot a bow and arrow at her.

Eddie had a big grin on his face when Emily turned back to the car.

"What's so funny freckles?" Emily enquired, not at all in the mood for jokes.

"Oh nothing," he replied mildly. "It's just great to have the real Emily back. I'm looking forward to whatever 'trouble' he might cause us" Eddie said in mocking tones.

Emily clearly didn't get (or want to get) his humour and brushed it aside as she returned to the car sullenly. "That's the problem with boys," she thought sadly to herself, "they're always looking for trouble."

The next few days were brilliant, regardless of Emily's conflicted feelings towards Eddie. They hardly saw Brent as he seemed to be camping with his family down at the lake and they were settled in a house in the village. On one occasion, whilst out boating, Eddie spotted

Brent practising with his big bow and arrow as they drove the boat past that end of the lake. Even from that distance, Eddie could tell Brent had a desire to show-off in front of the other kids. They purposely stayed away from him and spent most of their time out on the boat. It was awesome for all of them and even though Emily was trying her best to ignore Eddie, she had great fun jumping off the boat into the water and diving.

On the fifth day it was scorching hot with the sun beating hard. They could see the heatwaves rising as they looked down the long stretch of road to the lake. Once there they made themselves a brilliantly sheltered area in time for lunch. Then, while Pamela and Mom sat under the relative 'cool' of the trees, Jack, Eddie, and Emily set off again in the boat for the centre of the lake. This time they noticed a pair of jet ski were circling down near the end of the lake, where Brent's family was camping. Brent's dad had purchased a new jet ski and his uncle had bought one too. They were busy showing off their expensive new toys to the families on the lake and Brent, after much moaning and pestering, had convinced his dad to let him ride one by himself. Brent had a cunning idea. "I know exactly what to do," he chuckled mirthlessly. "I'll show them sissies. It'll be a great laugh to scare the knickers off that stuck up girl Emily" thought Brent, as he tried out a couple of tight circles on the jet ski. He had to build up his confidence as he didn't want to embarrass himself in front of those two knuckleheads again. Brent succeeded in making a few large waves with his ski. "That should do the trick!" he thought grimly to himself. "I might even knock them outta the boat!" he laughed devilishly as he practised closer to where Jack's boat was sitting. Eddie wasn't really taking any notice of Brent at all. He was too busy experimenting to see how deep he could dive. He wasn't the best diver, and the water was surprisingly cold only a few metres down from the surface. Emily was enjoying jumping off the roof of the little boat into the lake, so she also wasn't paying any attention to the jet ski (still a little way off) making interesting jerky movements in the water.

Jack noticed though. His eyes had been scanning the trajectory of the jet ski's progress. It looked like if it didn't change course soon, it would be coming straight for their boat. Jack wasn't too concerned though, as the jet ski and its rider didn't seem to be superbly confident, and the rider kept making small circles and almost tipping himself over from the waves he caused. The ski did keep coming closer though and before Jack had a chance to warn the two kids, Brent made a beeline for their boat and, as he came close, attempted to make one of his little circles to produce waves. Unfortunately, something went wrong, and Brent lost control of his steering at the last moment. The wave he was making pushed him nearer Jack's boat, the jet ski tipped, and Brent fell towards the side of the boat. Since Jack had been watching Brent, he couldn't see if Emily or Eddie were ok but without thinking twice, he rushed to the side of the boat with superhuman speed as Brent's head was just about to smack into the side rails of the boat, he jumped and held the jet ski back with one hand and Brent's chest with the other.

The impact of the fall was still quite significant, and Brent knocked his head slightly, causing him to pass out momentarily. Eddie was just coming up for air and Emily was staring in disbelief at what she had witnessed. As Jack had jumped to save Brent, the force of the wave's movement had rocked the boat enough for her to lose balance and fall into the lake. She was getting ready to jump anyway but had turned around at the noise of the jet ski. Emily had seen Jack's amazing speed as he literally stopped the jet ski from crushing Brent as it collided with the boat.

Eddie had missed the whole thing. Coming up for air, he was surprised to see Brent lying on the floor of the boat, looking ashen faced with shock and quite bewildered. Brent tried to get to his feet, wanting to check on his dad's jet ski but his legs were like jelly, and he had a funny dizzy feeling. He was not surprisingly finding it hard to think of the words to insult Emily. Luckily, someone had alerted Brent's dad and soon there was a jet ski riding out at speed to meet the boat. Jack had secured the jet ski safely (roped) to the rails after he'd lifted Brent into the boat. He must've been incredibly fast thought Emily. She'd never even noticed him retrieving the jet ski.

Brent's dad (Bob) was more than a bit upset and started swearing at his son for being reckless as soon as he came aboard. "You bloody idiot!" Bob shouted at the boy. "I'll clip your ears if you've scratched it".

"Excuse me sir," Jack spoke up, "I'm Jack. Eddie's father." He held out his hand politely to the aggressive man. Bob ignored the introduction and instead began looking intently at his jet ski for scratches.

"Ehem," Jack coughed loudly. "I think your son might have a concussion and may need urgent medical attention. Are you, his father?" Jack spoke with more authority this time, getting both Bob's attention and surprise. Bob had thought Brent was staying quiet and hiding on the floor of the boat to avoid a smack around the head from his old man, but when had a second look, he realised his mistake and decided to apologise.

"Oh, I'm sorry man. I thought my son was hiding away. He knows I'll give 'em a good learnin' if he crashes the bike" He held up his fingers to accentuate the word 'learnin' then went to the boy who was still a bit dazed and sheepishly trying to avoid his father's gaze.

"Ugh," Bob said gruffly, "you done it now haven't yer boy!" Bob was having difficulty conjuring up some empathy for his son in front of the strangers. Emily looked quite disgusted at the man, as he treated his son with such indifference. She had never seen someone treat a child like that.

"Well, we better get yer back to yer mom eh," Bob looked at the boy again. Brent was not going to be in any state to ride the ski back to shore. Bob had a predicament. He would have to get both back to shore by himself and he'd just made a fool out of himself in front of these strangers. He was trying to hide his embarrassment by covering it up with anger at his son. "What are ya gonna do now?! Ya can't ride it back can yer?!" mocking the boy harshly.

Jack intervened diplomatically. "No need to worry sir," Jack said to Bob. "We will tow the ski and Eddie will help get Brent and your ski back to shore."

A red-faced Bob accepted the offer with an awkward look.

"Well, I, urr.." Bob was struggling to thank Jack. "Yes, thanks for that" eyeing Brent with a scornful look. "I do hope we haven't caused too much trouble," Bob added politely, trying hard to act grateful.

Brent's shoulders lowered as the tension left; he looked equally relieved as he knew Jack had narrowly avoided a violent outburst from his dad. Some worry and embarrassment were still showing on Brent's face but he was hugely relieved at not having to ride back to shore.

"You don't have to be kind to me you know," he said sullenly to Emily when his dad had ridden off. "I'm not exactly your friend!"

Emily looked at Brent open faced and then with immense pity placed her hand on his shoulder. "It's ok Brent, no one's perfect," she winked at him, "But next time you wanna come swimming with us, just ask, ok?"

Brent smiled meekly back at Emily. Tears forming in his eyes.

And just like that, Emily had made a friend. A bully too. She punched him playfully on the shoulder to try and break the tension.

"You better not say sorry now that Jack saved your life" Emily smiled at Brent. He didn't return her smile. He was still embarrassed, dreading his father's 'discipline' and shocked at how nice they had been to him. No one had ever been that nice to him, especially people he didn't like. He shook his head in wonder as Eddie helped him out of the boat and onto the shore where his distressed mum was waiting for him. Jack had a few serious words with his parents about taking Brent to see a doctor to check out his head. Bob and his wife had an argument in front of everyone and Bob insisted there was nothing wrong with his son. In the end, Jack convinced Bob to at least take him to a doctor if he didn't improve in the next 24 hours. Bob agreed and everyone sighed with relief. As they left to go, Brent attempted to say something to Eddie and Emily.

"Ugh...... I mean..... Ummm. Hey guys, I really..." Brent stuttered. Eddie stopped him.

"Hey." Eddie winked. "See ya tomorrow". Brent smiled apologetically and let them go. He couldn't think of the words to say anyway.

As they boated back to the other shore, Emily stared thoughtfully at both Jack and Eddie and with a big smile, she faced Eddie. "You know, you might be an old bugger Ed, but I love ya to bits." She went over and hugged him tightly. Getting inside Eddie's brusque emotional exterior and breaking down those walls was a mighty task, but Emily had achieved enough for one day. He returned her heartfelt affection gladly.

"Friends?" he asked.

"Friends." she replied, tears now streaming down her face.

The next couple of days were a breeze. They went to check on Brent and he was doing remarkably well, although trying his best to use up all the available pity from his mum. Eddie asked if he'd like to come out on their boat. Brent accepted and they spent the remainder of their holiday laughing and diving and swimming on the lake together.

The three of them were the oddest collection of friends but they held a tremendous bond and Emily's quirky banter was equalled with Brent's sometimes harsh sarcasm. Eddie was a brilliant middle person for both, and they all became very good friends.

It looked as though this year at school would be a lot different to the last.

CHAPTER 05
ROYALS

Brian Parks had an idea. To him, it was a genius, fool-proof plan that no one would be able to work out. Brian had, of course, very little idea what a good plan might be, so his opinion of his cunning scheme was largely in his own head. In the great and long history of petty robbery, Brian's scheme would not be remembered as one of the all-time great heists. Unfortunately for Brian, it was what would come after his brilliantly executed break-in that would change the course of his life and, also unfortunately for Brian, it wasn't expected to favour him at all.

The Royals were due to arrive in Doon in a few weeks and Brian had chosen the timing of their visit to enact his plan. The plan (or sad attempt at one) was quite simple. Almost as simple as Brian.

It was to use the royal visit as a 'cover' for robbing a hunting store on the north side of the town, just past the botanic gardens. So where had this masterful idea emerged from? Brian had heard from some hunting buddies that the owner was going to shut up his shop for the day and join the many thousands of people planning to pour out into the streets to try and grab a view of one of the royal family. Brian's logic was simple; since all local police would be busy with the security arrangements for the visiting royals, none of them would be making any patrols. (Brian didn't know this for sure, in fact it was a gross underestimation of the local police force's ability, but he was absolutely sure that his guess was correct).

Just a couple of weeks before the royal visit, Brian had been riding shotgun in his mate's (Dan) ute. He was barely awake after Dan had ripped him from his bed at 5am to go hunting. Not that Dan had told him that yet, but Brian would find out soon enough.

"C'mon, Bri! Wake up man!" Dan laughed at Brian scornfully. "You look like you've never seen a sunrise, eh? City boyeeee!" Dan was laughing at Brian's expense, who had indeed agreed to be wrenched from his bed for a bit of early morning antics, however it was only Dan who was the one laughing at this stage.

As Dan drove along in the dark, Brian yawned again and peered through the early morning fog. He was now realising he had no idea where they were going.

"What's going on Dan? And why the hell did ya need to get me outta bed?" Brian tried to act as peeved as he could but inwardly, he was grateful to his strange buddy for prising him out of bed at this ludicrous hour. His life was sad and boring, and he desperately wanted something to do. Anything.

"Up for a bit o' hunting lad?" cheered Dan. Of course, Dan wasn't really asking, he was sort of more directing, such was the loud, brutish farmer boy type that he was. Dan was an old school friend of Brian's, who worked on a property not far up the peninsula from where Brian had grown up. His shaggy mop of curly blond hair and oversized thighs and arms poking out from a bush shirt and shorts was a stark contrast to the smaller, wiry trench coat wearing Brian who, if he was honest with himself, avoided physical activity whenever he could.

Dan could be persuasive though and had cajoled Brian into joining him on the early morning adventure. Brian groaned, he didn't like hunting, or walking long distances with those annoying dogs and he certainly didn't appreciate having to carry any dead animals back to the truck.

“Ugh! Ok Dan.” His tired resolve reluctantly giving way to Dan’s over-enthusiasm. “But I’m not carrying any stupid pigs, alright?!” Brian was playing hard to get, a little too hard.

“Fine by me laddy boy!” replied Dan, whilst lighting a cigarette skilfully for them both. “Me mum said I shouldn’t go alone into the bush anyway, but there’s free fags. You like free ciggies, dontcha?” Dan handed the lit cigarette to the now grateful and slightly more awake Brian.

Brian rolled his eyes as Dan turned the ute off the road up a driveway next to some shops.

“I’m just gonna get us some stuff for the trip, alright? You can wait here if you like but don’t let the boss man see you peeking in his store, ok?” Dan instructed Brian as he got out and headed for the rear door of the store. Brian couldn’t resist the bait his friend had given him.

“Not have a peek at the storeroom of a hunting store?!” Brian mused, laughing to himself. “No way! I’m not missing this!” So, Brian crept as best as he thought possible up to the supply door and whilst the clerk (a friend of his hunting mate) packaged up some supplies and ammunition for them, Brian had the great fortune to peek just inside the storeroom at the rear of the shop and glimpse the security sensors, locks and what-not. Mostly he noticed the power box. Like all hunting shops, this one had a secure vault for the dangerous firearms and ammunition, but it also had a security alarm. Brian saw both and began to devise a simple but (he thought) effective way to ensure he wouldn’t get caught if he visited the store again.

He could cut the power and since the owner would no doubt unlock the store in the morning (before the streets would fill up with people) and most likely leave the back gates unbolted for his return a few hours later, it would allow Brian access. It was a shot-in-the-dark plan, but Brian was uncannily quite astute in his presumption. On the day of the royal visit, the owner did instruct his store clerk to close the gates and just leave the chain unshackled, as surely no one would be sneaking around that day since everyone would be rubber necking down George Street trying for a peek at the princess.

In his defence, Brian hadn't planned on taking much from the store. His plan was just to take one of the large military-style hunting bags and fill it with some hunting equipment and, if he was lucky, a rifle from the cabinet. He knew there was little chance of getting any ammunition from the vault, so he concentrated on simply filling the bag with as much as he could. Many would wonder why he chose to waste such an opportunity to rob a store and not actually take much. Brian never stopped to consider things like that. To do those bigger jobs would require depending on other guys, probably as equally idiotic as he was! Nah, he liked to work alone. Less chance of messing things up, he convinced himself.

Brian was startled from his silent reverie with a shout from inside the store.

"Oi!" the clerk yelled at Dan. "Get your nosy friend outta here now! If the boss sees him, I'll be toast!" The clerk had noticed Brian's surreptitious peeking, but it was too late. Brian walked back to the ute, smiling from ear to ear. He was going to have a great day hunting and he didn't care a tosh about any dogs or if he was walking for miles, because Brian now had a plan.

So, on Wednesday the 27th of April, Brian set out early on his objective. He had to account for the thousands of extra people who also wanted to be in town that day, not to mention all the kids with the day off school so they could catch a glimpse of the royals too. Aside from a few overcrowded trams and buses though, his plan went remarkably well. With the back gate left unlocked, all he had to do was remove the fuses from the main switchboard but to Brian's exasperation, the power box had been padlocked shut. He wasted precious time banging the lock with rocks until the hinges broke and the cover fell off. Removing the fuses and placing them in his jacket, he then went to work on the rear door to the storeroom, all the while thinking it was some miracle that no one had caught him yet.

The door was no exception. If Brian had brought a sledgehammer with him, he might've achieved success far quicker but nonetheless, after quite a few attempts and with the help on an old steel fence post, he managed to break the door off its hinges and gain access to the storeroom. Such was the adrenaline surging though his veins and the excitement he was feeling coupled with the sweat from the exertion from all the bashing to get the door down, Brian was so wired and high from the experience that he didn't even check to see whether the alarm had a backup. Even stupid people can be lucky at times. Later that day, when the owner had returned to discover he'd been robbed and, after much yelling and cursing, he realised that the fault was partly his own, he discovered that he had seriously underestimated what even idiots like Brian would do to steal a bag of stuff.

Brian, after his initial surge of excitement and temptation to browse the aisles indefinitely (now that he felt bulletproof with confidence), successfully found the bag he desired and then proceeded to fill it with hunting jackets, knives, a compass, and binoculars. He stuffed the bag until it was bulging like a burrito, and he quickly became elated at his unexpected success. The adrenalin was making his heart pump fast; he hadn't felt this good since nabbing some diving gear from a poor soul's garage a week earlier. As he was walking back out through the storeroom, he noticed a box that the clerk must've forgotten to place in the vault. It was a brand new .338 Lapua!

"Pheweeee," Brian whistled through his teeth in astonishment. It was a genuine military-style sniper rifle. This sort of prize was far too seductive for Brian, and he quickly grabbed it out of the box and tried to fit it under his jacket. With great difficulty, he managed to 'hide' the rifle inside his jacket whilst carrying the massive bag over his shoulder. He didn't want anyone noticing his hidden weapon on his way home. Exalted, he walked as a giant would carry his plunder off down a street. People were walking back from the city centre in all directions and ignoring him. Brian now held a great feeling of invincibility. He was so sure that he would go unnoticed by everyone on his return home. He would be so wrong.

Brian was sauntering down towards the city, quite unnoticed by any one of the large throngs going to where the royals were meeting and greeting the locals. Many were walking past chattering excitedly about catching a glimpse of the famous couple and were still waving homemade royal memorabilia and Moray flags. It was a 20-minute walk through the town to the railway station where he was heading. By the time he arrived, he was a bit worn out and the adrenaline surge that had made him feel ecstatic before was all over and the bag felt heavy as did the rifle that by now was extremely uncomfortable to try and carry under his jacket.

He decided that he would hide behind the church across the intersection from the station, take out the rifle and rest for a few minutes before carrying on. Brian was about to intercept something a darn sight more uncomfortable than a rifle rubbing his chest the wrong way. He was about to encounter probably the worst day of his life.

A couple of hours earlier, in their secure bunker, Jack had been secretly instructing Eddie about the secure 'portals' he'd been developing over the course of the last few months. He was repeating to Eddie the importance of not 'jumping' with anyone else, lest it be too dangerous.

Over the past few months, Jack had been working on a secure hub for Eddie and himself to conduct their private meeting with Prince Dowling. The trouble wasn't finding a possible location close to King's High School, where the Prince and his entourage would be staying, but finding a place where the Prince could be alone. This needed to be for a sufficient period so as to have a worthwhile discussion about whatever it was the King had asked him to discuss. In the end, after much deliberation and 'too-ing' and 'fro-ing' with the Prince's royal guard, Sharma had instructed the Prince to visit a prominent cathedral, just a short walk from the main city centre. The choice to walk to the

First Church was a practical and reasonable alternative to some of other ideas proposed. (One idea was to 'jump' the Prince to a secure location and then 'jump him back, but they had to assume that the Prince would know nothing of their supernatural abilities so it couldn't be risked.)

The Prince would enter the church with a smaller entourage, leaving his wife (Princess Roslyn) for a few minutes to entertain the thousands of people cramming the city's streets. All eyes would be on his young wife as he simply stole five minutes away to conduct his father's business. The Prince would be escorted by his royal guard to the vestry behind the sanctuary, where they would secure the location and leave him alone in the room. Jack and Eddie, having spent some time organising the meeting, had met with the church's senior minister to calm any fears he might have over them doing 'business' with the future monarch in a holy place of prayer and worship. Jack had had to convince the minister they weren't up to anything 'ungodly' and had to submit 'oaths' and ritual prayers to confirm their innocence. It had been a stressful time keeping the minister happy. The royal guard was far more relaxed than the clergy and seemed happy to let the Prince handle the matter personally.

As Brian was leaving the hunting shop with his bag of goodies, Eddie shapeshifted into his 20-something self and, holding Jack's arm, 'jumped' instantaneously to the vestry room. It was perfectly timed to the second so that the minister would be greeting the Prince and his security guard in the foyer at the same time they jumped. The minister would have no idea of how they arrived but since he would be expecting them to be there, wouldn't be surprised to see them if he did, by chance, glance into the room when the Prince entered. The security guard would similarly be expecting to see them also and so wouldn't raise any alarms. And so, without any delay, the guards secured the room and left with the minister, and now the Prince and the Members were alone. They literally had five minutes. Whatever the Prince had to say, he needed to say it quickly.

Prince Dowling coughed nervously but immediately started proceedings in his usual manner

"Ahem, I do say. I bring my Kings gratitude that you could meet today masters Jack and Edward" said Prince Dowling nodding politely at them both separately. He was fastidiously well dressed, and his manners matched his elegance and humility given the tense situation. He was taller than Eddie remembered (it had been quite some time since he had last seen the Prince, probably when he was only a child) but the Prince did not acknowledge this, nor did he outwardly show any sign that he was perturbed by this awkward encounter. He merely took charge of the meeting and proceeded to deliver his message with acute precision. To Eddie's relief, the Prince didn't recognise Eddie at all. Sensing his duty to his father and to the task he was charged with, the Prince spoke first.

"My King requests that I forego our most common decencies of introductions, as of course we have little time with which to conduct our business."

Both Eddie and Jack nodded to the Prince silently, allowing him to continue uninterrupted.

"I thank you," remarked the Prince with ludicrous formality, almost as if he was miming. Eddie and Jack both knew that the Prince was exceptionally well-mannered and well-spoken so weren't at all surprised by his remark.

Clearing his throat, the Prince set about conveying his private message. He didn't seem to be in a hurry; he didn't rush his words or stop to repeat. He had memorised the message in its entirety and made no mistakes. He truly was an expert. His father had chosen well.

"The Moray Kingdom has been compromised in intelligence and trade. Our hope of future dominance in the region is over. From West Quaran to the trade routes of the Nina and from Eridu to Sharan, we have been betrayed. Neither do we know who our *enemy* is, only that (emphasis added), like before, *they* have a common enemy, the Indami."

The Prince paused for a moment then continued.

"Again, it seems *they* try to draw the Kingdom into a war so that we will fight their enemies. We will risk no such conflict."

Facing Eddie, the Prince squared his attention and speech at him directly. "Edward, Jack. friends and confidants, to save our kingdom from ruin we must know who conspires against us in secret. Whoever it is that moves to draw us to engage in *their* conflict has already engaged that fool Sperre to invade Mera."

Mera was a small coastline kingdom which neighboured one of their most fragile of allies, Indami. Mera was often used by the enemies of Indami to draw Moray and their allies into destructive wars, usually by disrupting trade but mostly weakening the Indami. Sperre was a hardened military man but also now the current leader of Indami and had launched an unprecedented campaign against their foes in Mera. It was a disaster for both countries.

Facing them both again the Prince continued.

"Why do *they* seek to draw us into their conflict? Is it to further weaken our position? We need to know what silent partner benefits from this charade. All of this I, the King, ask in the highest of secrecy giving you, Edward, the highest honour and the trust of my closest confidant, my son, the Prince. To this end, I request at the earliest possible convenience, plans to meet again to discuss your findings to these worrisome events."

The Prince finished and gave a moment of silence to the pair so they could take in the full message. It was a lot to comprehend.

Not surprisingly, the Prince was taken aback when Edward responded abruptly to this highly sensitive request.

"My Prince," Eddie spoke as formally as he could manage, "Neither Jack nor I will permit such an investigation." He looked sadly back at the Prince who was noticeably knocked off his well-tuned 'always' calm appearance.

"But you must!" blurted out the Prince in astonishment. He could hardly believe what he was hearing. The young man was denying a direct request from the King on the highest possible security threat.

Ignoring his distress, Jack spoke plainly to Prince. "My Lord Prince, Edward is right. we cannot do that which you ask. For the King to put his trust in us is a high honour indeed and is not taken lightly. However, I can only say that we have been trying for decades now to discover the intentions of these 'silent' partners you speak of.

"Silent partners we know nothing of, but we do know some of the intentions of your common enemy and one of them in particular is the removal of El Ami and the Indami peoples," Jack finished and fell silent, waiting for the Prince's response. Getting none, he continued

"My prince, it is no small feat of honour that you have shown such mercy towards the Indami now for decades. It surely has been the deciding factor in warding off many large-scale attempts to annihilate them and drive them from their land. That the Indami have grown more powerful in the last decade is proof that your support of their nation has succeeded.

Eddie let Jack fall silent for a moment and sensing the pause he finished for Jack.

"My Lord Prince, your enemies grow not because of your weakness but because of the strength of El Anil in the region. Mera and their cabal of warlords are sabre rattling to see what you do." Eddie felt the need to rush now, sensing that time was running out. Clearly the Prince was not going to get the answer he desired. Eddie and Jack would have to reassure him somehow. He continued as the Prince winced at what he heard.

"El Anil is the bait the draws out the enemies of the free world. For their sake we must wait for them to make a mistake that exposes their true intentions.

"Strengthen your ally and force this 'Silent Partner' to make the first move!" Eddie finished firmly.

Eddie cringed inwardly for the Prince. It was extremely difficult to arrange these meetings let alone try to discuss matters of global security in under five minutes, plus they had more than likely given him the least useful answer.

Perhaps the Prince knew how preposterous the likelihood of his meeting with Eddie and Jack being a success, yet his exasperation at Eddie's refusal to investigate for his King was a genuine crack in an otherwise perfect display of calm. Prince Dowling no doubt had much more responsibility in foreign affairs than he conveyed in public, so his brief outburst accentuated his frustration when compared to his more natural civil tones.

Eddie knew how tough it was for the young Prince and even though most of the world had benefited enormously from almost four decades without large scale military conflict, their Kingdom had completely changed in that time. Entire countries which used to be part of the Empire were now independent nations and the Crown itself was no more than a figurehead. The war may have stopped for King Melville, but the conflict had not. It had merely changed from swords and gunships to lawyers and politicians.

Melville had warned his son to be wary of the old powers who ruled the trade routes, especially the Nina-controlled waters where a trade embargo could threaten all global trade. Eddie knew the Prince feared something much worse than an embargo at Nina, so felt that Dowling at least deserved an explanation of some kind. Something that might buy them some time yet also covertly encourage the King and somehow alleviate any misguided fears.

Eddie had to reach out to the Prince. He knew there was little time to convey any reason for their decision. Eddie needed to do something that only King Melville would understand. Something that they both understood far more than words. Eddie reached into his jacket pocket and pulled out an old silver teaspoon that had an image like a souvenir picture of a building on the tip of its handle. If you looked closely, you could just make out an engraving in the shape of an apple.

Eddie stared at the spoon for a moment, then, with a look of fierce determination, offered it to the Prince.

At first the Prince was startled by this unusual offering. He eyed Eddie with intense curiosity, as if by observing Eddie he might elicit some meaning to the strange gift.

"My Lord Prince," Eddie said, as he presented the spoon like an expensive watch. "Please give this to King Melville. He alone knows the meaning of this. Only he will understand. I can assure you it will be a huge help to him."

The Prince looked puzzled for a moment, then seemed to inwardly consider something, then he briefly glanced at his watch and regained his composure. He spoke with his confidence and purpose returned now. He didn't mean to linger with persuasive arguments for his King nor did he seek to advocate on his behalf.

"My King thanks you my friends, as do I." The Prince spoke politely. "I must depart now. Know that you have your majesty's full trust, in the same as you hold the hope in his heart that he has in yours.

"I hope to see you both again my friends." He managed a courteous smile.

And with that, the Prince left the room the way he came in. It had barely been any time at all since he had entered the room but seemed much longer. Strange how time seems to stretch when something important or terribly exciting is happening. Eddie was grateful for the haste of the audience with the Prince and was equally grateful to Jack for backing him up so promptly when it was obviously a huge deal.

They would talk about it later. Right now, it was imperative that they leave as soon as possible. Jack didn't hesitate and disappeared instantly before anyone could enter the room. Eddie thought immediately of

Emily who was waiting patiently behind the church for Eddie whilst they had their meeting with the Prince. Emily didn't know what they were there for, she didn't ask either. The minister seemed like a boring old fart anyway and Emily wasn't the least bit interested. Eddie said they were only going to be five minutes and Emily still had a few chapters of her favourite book to finish so she was happy to wait. She was hoping they might be able to see one of the royals while they were in town on their day off school together. She sat there quietly engrossed in her book. It would take a few moments for Eddie to change back to his 10-year-old self before departing the church.

So quiet and still was Emily that a young man in an oversized jacket and carrying a big bag walked stealthily round to almost where Emily was sitting. She was up on some stone steps that led to the rear door of the vestry, and the man was slightly out of ear shot so unless she glanced that way, he probably would've gone unnoticed. Brian however needed to get the rifle out because it was causing him considerable discomfort. Unfortunately for Brian, he didn't notice that he was making quite a few loud grunting noises and letting off some choice swear words that I'm sure Emily has never heard before. Ever. In the few seconds that it took for Brian to free the large rifle from his jacket, Emily had noticed the loud grunting sound accompanied by the cursing and her head turned to see what all the fuss was about. At that very moment, Eddie opened the vestry door and Brian stood there, having finally liberated the weapon. His eyes and Eddie's became transfixed in amazement.

Almost a second went by before anything happened. As usual, Eddie saw things happen in a sort of slow-motion frame-by-frame way, which made the event feel like it lasted much longer. As Emily stared at the young man holding the rifle, she was completely frozen and utterly speechless watching the spectacle. Before Emily or Eddie could react however, there was a loud bang, like a pistol being fired.

A look of terror came over Brian's face, but he wasn't looking at Eddie. His focus was on something coming towards him from the other side of the church. Brian panicked and immediately ran off towards the station, absentmindedly carrying the rifle and leaving the bag next to the steps.

As Eddie and Emily's gaze met, unaware of the person Brian had seen, they were both about to break into a nervous laugh when they heard another shot. This time it sounded like a real pistol and a lot closer.

Coming from the opposite direction was an elderly looking man stumbling towards Eddie holding a pistol clumsily in his hand. Emily, for the first time since the whole debacle started, shrieked loudly in fright. Eddie's amusement turned to panic and forgetting centuries of self-control and training under Jack and Sharma, grabbed Emily's arm and jumped.

Except he couldn't jump. Not properly anyway. He had intended to jump them both the short distance to an abandoned part of the railways not far off, but somehow the old man had caught the trail and jumped with them. Eddie was terrified now. This man was clearly trying to kill either himself or Emily and seemed to have considerable powers. And he had a mighty weapon. Eddie attempted to jump again. This time he tried to make it to the Gardens.

It was a bad decision but, in his panic, Eddie chose any place he could think of and didn't consider the planning that Jack had taught him.

This time it was slow. Really slow. Usually when he jumped it was instantaneous, but this time it was a much slower version of flying. He heard another shot being fired as they crossed the northern grounds of the university. That old man was following him?! Eddie didn't know what to do. He had to save Emily but there was no way he could even attempt to try to jump to one of their safe houses with this old guy trailing behind his jump.

How did the old man follow where he was going? And how was he able to slow his movement down like that? Eddie's thoughts were not working properly either. He tried his best to focus on Emily and what they would do when they got to the gardens, but he was struggling to concentrate, and Emily didn't appear to be doing at all well herself. The initial shock of the pistol shot and then the abrupt movement of Eddie jumping them had made her feel like she had vertigo. Now that they both realised the old man was trailing them towards the gardens, Emily was about to become hysterical with fear. She didn't though. Eddie's stern face was incredibly powerful to her. She couldn't tell that he was panicking himself. To her, he seemed like he was in control, and she placed her trust in him. Eddie didn't feel at all sure of himself, but he knew that he couldn't let this old guy get to them. He'd have to figure out a way somehow.

Eddie and Emily both gasped in relief.

He didn't know if it was blind luck or mere coincidence but for the first time ever, he was grateful to see Evantine.

Eddie didn't get a chance to ask how Evantine had managed to figure out they needed help because they were running out of time. Soon they'd make it to the gardens and would have to make another jump. They would also have to risk the possibility that the old man would jump with them again and most likely fire off a shot or two when he got in shooting range. Eddie saw Evantine just as they entered the gardens. The old man now was trailing them by 150 yards and getting closer. Soon he would be able to shoot directly at them, although, going by his previous shots, at closer range he hadn't had any success at all. Eddie didn't really perceive his own faulty logic at the time as he was too panicked and far too fearful to be rational and objective in the circumstance. When he got to Evantine, the Nord spoke to them hurriedly. Pointing towards one of the utility buildings nearby. Evantine seemed in complete control.

"Go now, through that storeroom door. I have made a temporary portal."

Eddie glanced a worried look towards the Nord.

The Nord seemed to restrain himself and with great care, calmly spoke to them. "It is safe for both of you, but you must go now.

Do not fear the old man; I will despatch our enemy. Now go!" He commanded them.

They hurried to the door and rushed through the portal as the Nord charged after the old man still flying towards them.

In an instant, breathless and shivering in shock, Eddie and Emily stumbled out into a hilltop area far from the city. It was windy and cold up there which did little to alleviate their already frayed nerves. It took a few moments for Eddie to realise where they were. When he did, he let out a groan of frustration.

Evantine had jumped them far away from danger but had also jumped them far away from any place useful. Plus, Eddie didn't feel at all confidant in trying to jump again just in case it failed. He didn't need that kind of risk and there was a large harbour in between where they stood and home.

From where they stood, they were on the north side of the harbour, far above the port. From there you could almost see all the head and the peninsula and if you walked a few minutes around the slope, you could look down on the city, a few miles to the south. It was a beautiful sight and had they both been able to enjoy the view, they both would've probably been enthralled by it, since they loved exploring the outdoors.

But Emily was freezing and frightened and Eddie was dealing with a huge internal conflict that he couldn't discuss with Emily. It wasn't a particularly warm day and part of the reason why she hadn't been too keen to stand in the city streets waiting for a glimpse of the princess was it was likely to rain. Emily just didn't see the logic in wasting her time to peek at some overdressed 'pretty girl' waving at a bunch of strangers anyway.

"Ed, I'm fr, fr, freezing up here," she said, her teeth chattering. "I love a mountain walk just as much as you do................." Emily said, trying to find some humour somewhere to distract Eddie as he didn't seem to know what to do.

Eddie was indeed struggling with what to do. Evantine had jumped them out of the way. Why hadn't he jumped them to his home?

Was there a danger there also? Could their home be compromised? Did Evantine know something he didn't? Eddie's mind was running with terrible thoughts and the shock and cold were not helping at all. When Emily spoke, it helped him focus on their immediate problem and her attempt at humour was both surprising and comforting.

"I'm sorry Em," said Eddie now trying to smile at her weak joke. "I don't know how we got here, and I don't know if we should try to get back..." His voice trailed as his mind again tried to find something that could help them.

Emily noticed a path leading behind them into a dense forest that went back down the hill. Sensing that Eddie wasn't going to make any decisions anytime soon, she pulled him after her and took the lead.

"C'mon Ed," she said, now taking control of her shivering and trying to be assertive. "Let's walk down there. The walk will warm us up and there's no wind down there, right?"

Eddie nodded to her. She was right, the walk would do them good. They would get warm and while they walked down the lengthy track through the forest, they discussed what had happened and tried to make sense of it. Eddie was amazed at Emily. She didn't seem scared now and in some sense the situation had made it possible for her to be assertive and make decisions when Eddie couldn't.

"Ed, do you think that old man was trying to shoot at you?" Emily asked.

"Yeah, I don't know," said Eddie, "but he was definitely a shapeshifter."

Emily punched him in the arm jokingly. "I've never seen you 'that' scared Ed," she said. "You had me really worried."

"I AM worried Em." He replied thoughtfully, ignoring her taunt. "What if I can't jump us back to safety?" His mind once again desperately trying to find a way. Then it came to him. The Portals!

"Yes!" he exclaimed loudly. Grinning, he turned to her and shouted. "The portals!"

With a look of confusion, Emily tried to question Eddie as to what he meant by 'portals' but she didn't get a chance because Eddie had grabbed Emily's arm and jumped them to a remote hillside overlooking the ocean. Eddie had been there a few times before with Jack. They stood outside the derelict old, ruined remains of a very old farm house. This was the Portal that Jack had brought Eddie to months ago. This was also portal that he had warned Eddie not to try and jump from with anyone. Ever. But Eddie had an idea. No one knew where they were and if Emily was right, then the old man had been trying to kill him and not Emily, so she was safe at least.

If Eddie used the portal to safely return to the house alone, he could check to see whether it was safe and then return with help to retrieve Emily. Leaving a 10-year-old girl in a remote coastal farm alone, where no one knew where she was or how to get in contact was quite a risky venture, especially if Eddie was held up in any way, or worse.

"You want to leave me here!" she shot back at Eddie after he had explained his plan. "What will I do? How long will you be?"

For the first time, tears started to well in her eyes. Perhaps the fear of being left alone was too much. Maybe the uncertainty of whether Eddie would return was too much for her or whether the shock and tiredness had finally caught up with her, she didn't know but felt overwhelmed by it and almost instantly was apologising to Eddie.

"It's ok Em," comforted Eddie as much as he could. "I'm sorry too. Again, it's my fault for getting us into all this mess and you always end up in the thick of it!"

"I'm such a blubber baby!" Emily retorted. "Crying like a little girl who's lost her doll."

"You're THE bravest girl I know Em," he replied, a look of fierce determination on his face as he struggled to hold down his own troubles. He didn't know what to do. He didn't want to leave Emily if she felt unsafe, but he also needed to make sure their home wasn't compromised either. It was a conundrum he was having great difficulty resolving. Eddie had also not taken much notice of how much time had passed since they had left the church. He drew a sharp breath when he finally glanced at his watch. It was already past 3pm! Now the added pressure of time was against them as was the brisk sea air coming in from the coast only a short distance away.

They weren't just shivering from the cold, however.

They were startled by the sound of movement inside the ruined building and Eddie rush to grab Emily just in case it was the old man. Just as he was about to grab her and jump to anywhere, he could instinctively think of, Jack appeared in the broken doorway of the farmhouse looking frightful and clearly in shock himself. When he saw Eddie and Emily, he reacted quite out of character and let out a loud shout.

"Yes! I found you!" Jack bellowed, stunning them both momentarily.

He ran up and wrapped his arms around them. Hugging them tight, he didn't know if it was for his benefit or theirs. After the initial surprise at seeing Jack, the two kids both laughed and whatever Emily's fears had been before instantly vanished when she saw Jack. Eddie wasn't quite so comforted by Jack's sudden appearance but was noticeably impressed and enormously grateful to see his friend.

"Jack," Eddie questioned him, "how on earth did you know where to find us?"

"It wasn't easy," he replied earnestly. "When you didn't return home with Emily, I panicked and returned immediately to the church."

Jack then explained to them the confusion of seeing a dozen police officers and royal guard forces all very busily investigating a scene at the rear of the church. He conveyed to the kids that he didn't risk hanging around to see what had happened just in case one of the royal security attachés recognised him accidently, so he'd immediately jumped to another location to start searching for them. Before he jumped, he'd seen a young man being arrested and thrown quite literally into a police van by a large police officer who Jack could only guess was a detective.

"Pheweeeeeeee!" Emily whistled in astonishment. "They must've thought the young man was going to try to shoot the princess!"

"He was hiding a rifle in his jacket!" she cried. Eddie looked at her in surprise, finally realising the irony of the situation.

"They never saw the old man, did they?" Eddie interjected excitedly. "They think the shot came from that young guy!" He stared back at Emily in amazement when he had pieced together the bits of the story.

Jack was confused by their interruptions. Old man? Rifle? Shot? What was going on? Jack looked at Emily and Eddie in disbelief. The situation was much worse than he had imagined; quite possibly there had been an attempt to kill either Eddie or Emily and it had come entirely by surprise yet there they stood on a remote coastal paddock in what seemed like relative safety. Ignoring what he couldn't understand for now, Jack tried to focus on explaining to Eddie and Emily how he got there.

"I checked ALL the portals Ed." Jack spoke seriously to Eddie now. "I couldn't find you! I was about to panic, then I thought perhaps you might try to bring Emily back through this portal if you were desperate."

Eddie's eyes widened in amazement at how much Jack had assumed he might be prepared to risk. Jack stopped him before Eddie could jump to conclusions.

"I knew you would never do something that dangerous Ed, you're far too cautious," winking at Emily, "and Emily is far too smart to let you be that stupid."

Emily kicked Jack in the shins playfully.

"Eddie has been amazing Jack!" she responded in abrupt defence of Eddie. "That old guy was SHOOTING at us!" she shouted at Jack.

Not knowing whether Emily was being serious or not, Jack sent a mute appeal to Eddie. Jack was having a hard time piecing together the events that had transpired and wasn't at all understanding how they'd ended up at the most remote portal only Eddie and himself knew about.

"Jack," Eddie questioned Jack seriously now. "Are we safe here? I want to tell you what happened to us, but we must do it somewhere safe and we both know that Emily can't travel through this portal."

Jack realised the problem only too well and nodded his head at Eddie. Beckoning them into the old ruin where the wind wasn't quite so strong, he whispered to them.

"There is one portal that we can take Emily with us to, but it will be perilous if the wrong people have already guessed what we might do next. Considering today's events, we have been extremely lucky not to have lost one of you. If this 'Old Man' knew to attack you before, he might easily try it again."

Jack didn't know about the help that Evantine had given them in the gardens. Eddie did his best to tell Jack quickly how the Nord had assisted them to escape the old man. A look of intense suspicion came over Jack when Eddie told him this. Jack was quickly realising how the situation had become even more confusing.

"Evantine has gone after the old man," Eddie informed his friend. "He sent us to some hilltop probably thinking it was a safe option."

"It was bloody stupid!" Emily butted in rudely. After blushing, then recovering from blurting out her unexpected curse, she tried explaining. "He could've sent us home, right?"

Jack pondered what both the children had said and stood there quietly for a few moments longer, thinking it over. It was amazing that Eddie had the good sense to jump them to this remote location as only himself and Ed knew of it but everything else from the day's events frightened him. They had been totally unprepared for such danger, and it seemed only by sheer luck that Evantine had been able to assist them to safety, albeit a strange one.

Looking to Emily he said softly "The Nord may have sent you somewhere of much less danger than you can presume. He could not at the time assume that home was safe."

Looking to Eddie, he seemed to have gathered himself and his confidence had visually returned by the time he addressed the young boy.

"Ed, if Evantine has gone after this 'Old Man' then we can all but guarantee the Nord has achieved success in this and there is absolutely no way he would compromise the safety of our home."

"Emily, with your permission, I will accompany you to our home by making the necessary jumps with you to avoid any dangers along the way," Jack stated, then turned to Eddie.

"Eddie," Jack spoke to him directly, very quietly, almost in a whisper, "You must find the Prince and make sure that he is safe and find out if the attack was meant for him. Then you must find the Sharma and return with him to the house."

"Do not return to the house without Sharma!" Jack insisted. "He may be the protection you need if we have been found." Glancing at his watch, he made some mental calculations then added a caveat.

"Four hours should give you plenty of time," Jack impressed upon Eddie. "If you have not returned then, we will assume the Sharma, or you have been compromised and we will get Emily to safety immediately."

They both looked darkly at each other, knowing what "compromised" could mean. It was a serious undertaking. They might not see each other again and Eddie knew he could trust Jack to do the right thing and protect Emily even if that meant leaving Eddie to fend for himself. If they hadn't felt the seriousness of the situation before, they did now and Eddie's troubled glances towards Emily acknowledged his fears. Noticing this, Jack held the younger man's shoulder tightly, trying to convey a sense of courage and trust. Eddie returned the older man's affection with a half-hearted attempt at a cheeky wink, then bade them both a grim goodbye.

Before they could leave however, Emily insisted on hugging Eddie until both Eddie and Jack had to prise her off. Tears streaming down her face she pulled herself together to punch Eddie in the arm.

"Don't be a hero Ed," Emily tried to lighten the weight of the guilt she felt for him having to leave. But mostly she wanted him to be safe.

"You know they can't do diddly squat without you, so you'd better be careful!" Emily blurted out to Eddie, her heart in her mouth just as Jack took her arm and jumped them to their next destination. Jack wasn't particularly interested in long goodbyes, especially when the threat of danger was fast becoming a possibility. Eddie knew Emily would be safe with Jack and the choice to send Eddie back to investigate was a clever one, yet problematic considering the Nord had forbidden Eddie from doing such tasks.

Eddie groaned with internal frustration as he tried to plan out his mission. Getting to the Prince sounded easy, but it might be a trap. What if the first meeting was intended to be a trap? If it was, had it succeeded or failed?

And, if it was a trap, then who was the target? Was it him? Emily? The Prince? Eddie needed to find answers and fast. No doubt the Royals and their security would have great interest in the day's events too. Eddie couldn't rule out the possibility that the Prince might've suspected that Eddie and Jack were drawing the Prince into a trap.

"That's crazy talk Ed," he mumbled to himself. "They contacted us, remember?!" Eddie groaned within himself again, before gathering up enough courage to decide where to jump first.

He decided to jump for the Prince's brother, Calton. Using his skills, he would be able to overhear any discussions relating to Prince Dowling. If found, he would merely be a stranger and would have a greater chance of shapeshifting and jumping somewhere else without creating too much fuss.

Finding Sharma was going to be far more difficult, and he had very little time. He was going to have to hope the Sharma was as wise as Eddie suspected and would find him first.

Hungry and cold, Eddie stood there for a few moments to try and collect his thoughts as best he could. Jack and Emily had gone, the emptiness of the landscape resembling the sudden alienation he felt. He stood there alone, looking down the hillside at the ocean. Emily was safe and Jack had by some miracle worked out what Eddie was thinking and come to his aid. He knew that Jack would look after Emily and so now he focused his mind to gather the courage he would need. He would have to go out there on his own and quite possibly put himself in greater danger than before. If the Prince had been the intended victim, then it was certain that Eddie would be walking into danger and the second task of finding Sharma could be equally as problematic if the Sharma was the real target. Biting his lip unconsciously, Eddie gulped down his fear and groped internally for his confidence. He wasn't about to let his friends down and Jack had proven to be a faithful friend.

So, bravely facing an uncertain future, he thought of his friend Emily and how she needed his help. The Prince also might need his help. Sharma might need his help. Jack certainly needed it. Pushing aside his fear, he made up his mind. He would do it for them. Focusing King's High School in his mind, he turned around and faced back towards the city far away miles to the south and jumped.

CHAPTER 06
DETAINED

As Brian emerged from the back of the church, he was met by a startled Matt Ferguson, who looked as equally surprised as he was. Earlier that day, Matt had been ordered by his captain to drive around the inner city (as much as the crowds would allow) because his bosses wanted to make it seem like the whole place was swarming with police to impress the royals. Matt thought this was ridiculous but went along with it as it meant for an easy day, and he secretly hoped to catch a glimpse of one of the royals himself or even perhaps get an autograph for his niece and nephew who couldn't make the journey to Doon to see them.

When Matt heard the shots fired, he thought like everyone else that some idiot was playing silly games in their cars, backfiring their engines to try and scare the throng of people walking up and down the city's main boulevards and waiting for a glimpse of Princess Roslyn. There were hundreds of people spewing out into the side streets so that now people were taking up most of the roads. It was Matt's job to try and encourage them back onto the sidewalk. When he had made it a block back from the city square, he was almost at the church grounds where, unbeknownst to him, a secret meeting was taking place. Aside from the unusual amount of foot traffic, there had been little trouble so as he turned the corner behind the church he was startled by the loud sound.

Looking around, Matt quickly devised that no car had made that sound, but he was more than surprised when Brian emerged, panic stricken from the back of the church carrying a rifle, because Brian seemed just as scared and as startled as Matt was.

It only took Matt an instant to notice that the rifle had no cartridge and appeared to be partially disabled, however his training kicked in and he immediately took protective evasive action in case Brian was carrying a second weapon. Although Brian didn't happen to be carrying the rifle in a position that one might carry it when about to fire, Matt didn't hesitate or take any chances. He ran immediately from the patrol car and tackled Brian to the ground before Brian could respond.

Breathless, winded from being knocked to the ground and dizzy from where his head had hit the pavement, Brian tried to ask Matt what on earth he was doing, but before he could get his thoughts together his wrists were handcuffed behind his back. There seemed to be at least 2 or 3 other officers already standing around, trying to make some sense of the supposed shots fired.

"Hey! Whadda yur doin? Yer blimin &%$#! asshat" Brian managed to shout at Matt who currently had him pinned face down on the sidewalk.

But Matt wasn't about to take any chances with Brian and his adrenaline was pumping. He didn't know if he believed that Brian had shot the rifle, but his training had set in, and he had to do his job. After quickly disarming him and checking for 'other' weapons he checked the rifle. Brian had been wielding a powerful hunting rifle. loaded or not, Brian was dangerously close to where Matt most definitely suspected there to have been gunshot sounds.

Matt wrestled the frightened young man to the ground with surprising force. Brian didn't stand a chance against Matt's rugby tackle and quick thinking. Whilst Matt had Brian down on the cold pavement, he barked at Brian for answers. "Is there another weapon Brian?" Matt demanded, whilst forcing Brian's shoulder hard into the ground.

Quickly scanning the area, Matt considered his options. "Find out if there's another shooter you two!" he commanded the two officers standing there looking quite apprehensive. They had never been tasked with securing a firearms scene before but obeyed Matt's orders and headed in the direction Brian had come. As they made their uneasy walk towards the vestry, Matt returned his attention to Brian. He knew that whilst Brian looked innocent, appearances can often be deceiving so he didn't hesitate and pushed Brian's shoulder as hard as he deemed acceptable into the footpath. Although he dreaded what might happen if certain 'other' senior officers arrived, he didn't have much time.

"C'mon Brian!" pleaded Matt, "soon the big wigs will be here, and you'll be screwed alright?!" Matt was trying desperately to reign in his surge of adrenaline so he could keep a clear head. He needed answers and he needed them quickly before

"Found a bullet! Looks like 9 millimetre!" One of the supporting officers yelled out to Matt.

Not at all having any progress on calming himself down Matt felt powerless and exposed. If there *was* another shooter, then they could've disappeared into the crowds easily by now.

"I ain't got no blimin pistol so you can piss off aww right!" Brian tried to shout at Matt with his face hard against the ground and fighting through the pain in his face and shoulder. Matt didn't believe him at all, yet Brian had been carrying a rifle that was not in any operational state either. Doubt was creeping in, but he tried to remember his training and knew he had to keep Brian talking. Thankfully that wasn't too hard.

"I don't know who fired the shot! OKAY!" Brian managed to rasp out. Difficult considering Matt's full body weight was currently pinning him down.

"Hardly believable story Bri" Matt scorned him mercilessly.

"What on earth are you doin' carrying a rifle in the centre of town Brian?" Matt asked, hardly believing he was asking such an outrageous question. Was Brian *THAT* stupid he would walk through town with a rifle on possibly the busiest day in Doon's history?!

A second officer called out that another bullet had been found near the vestry rear doorsteps.

Matt kept his knee on Brians shoulder as if it helped him focus his mind on the task at hand. He was grateful there was other officers now beginning to arrive on the scene. It was a huge help to Matt but had the opposite effect on Brian. He was absolutely stunned by how quickly the situation had gone from bad to worse. One moment he was rearranging his jacket and the next he was getting shot at.

Utterly confused by the disappearance of the old man with the pistol he couldn't understand how he could've escaped. Growing more distraught and bewildered by the moment, Brian knew he better shut his mouth now before he made it worse. Every cop in Doon would be absolutely convinced that Brian had fired those shots and somehow hid the weapon.

Whatever stopped Brian from talking, Matt could not understand but he was unable to get anything out of the young man. Brian refused to speak even with a dozen or so officers standing around in a menacing way. All until Lewis turned up at the scene. Lewis had got there fast too. In fact, due to the high security nature of the royal visit and the fact that most of the local police were bored stiff, most of the cops in the vicinity had run to the church just for something to do and because their wives would mock them for weeks if they didn't get an eye-witness account of the 'sniper'.

Detective Lewis just happened to be organising a security detail for Prince Calton (prince Dowling's younger brother) and was only a couple of blocks away when he heard an alert on one of the constable's radios. He stopped the meeting short and literally ran for the church in his trench-coat. By the time he got to Matt he was disappointed at seeing Brian in cuffs already and even more displeased that Matt was trying to shuffle him into his patrol car.

"No, you don't mate." Lewis shouted with alarming authority at Matt, instantly getting the attention of all the on-duty policemen 'investigating' the supposed crime. "He's coming with me before you can let the little punk off and get him home to mummy!"

Matt stopped and eyed up the taller, more senior officer. For a moment it looked as if Matt was considering defying Lewis. Instead, he deferred to his superior officer and Matt shoved young Brian hard towards Lewis. If Lewis was offended in any way, he didn't show it, apart from a grin that had begun to form on Lewis's face as the older detective seemed to be enjoying the obvious provocation. "Just you wait Ferguson," thought Lewis to himself, "you'll get what's coming to ya". Lewis didn't react verbally to Matt's jibe and just stared at him, waiting for an answer, as they shoved Brian into the patrol car.

"Fine," Matt replied sardonically. "But just so you know, the other officers couldn't find another shooter OR a weapon and Brian's rifle is useless." Lewis's eyes widened in disbelief, but his curiosity got the better of him.

"Well, well," Lewis replied nastily. "It's a mystery we have then, is it?". Lewis's cynicism was for show, but he was profoundly grateful for the afternoon's events as it gave him a decent excuse to get away from the boredom of babysitting a dozen royal attendants. It looked as if his afternoon just kept on getting better and better, thanks to Matt and this idiot boy, Brian.

"Perhaps there is more here than just a stupid prank" Matt pointed to the handcuffed Brian, secured in the patrol car. Matt was painfully right of course, and Lewis knew it too. Lewis had risked hurting his reputation by acting recklessly towards Ferguson, so he decided to change tack with Matt and assuage the younger officer. "You are of course a first responder and will be submitting evidence as such?" Lewis grudgingly asked Matt, offering a morsel of cooperation.

Matt wasn't going to let Lewis rule the scene without taking some concessions and by now he was overly suspicious about the whole ordeal. Matt tried his luck.

"I'll be joining you as co-investigator for questioning the lad." He shot Lewis and then Brian a scornful look. "Wouldn't say anything. Quiet as a mouse, he is!"

Lewis drew a wicked smile of contentment from what Matt had said. Matt had thought the older officer would resist having him there as an interviewer, but Lewis was cunning. By engaging Matt in the investigation, there was a much higher chance of getting a real confession out of the boy. Lewis was feeling the elation of finally having something worthwhile and interesting to do for the day, besides babysitting those boring royal muppets. He was practically singing with joy behind his scornful visage.

"Ok, Matt." Lewis replied acidly with a huge false grin. "Let's have it your way then, shall we?"

Lewis directed one of the other officers to get in the police station wagon so they could at least get Brian hidden away as quickly as possible. There were already a few people milling around, rubber necking to see what all the fuss was about, and Lewis didn't want too many loose lips before he had a chance to soften Brian up in private.

The quick thinking from Lewis was a stroke of genius. With Brian tucked away from peering eyes, people would get bored standing around. Nobody knew what was happening and none of the police even knew if it was anything more than a false alarm. Lewis was adept at shutting scenes down and ordering officers to "Get back to work!"

Within an hour, most of the police had moved away, but a couple of plain clothes forensics staff had been called in to check for bullets and residue. Lewis may have been an arrogant and narcissistic man, but he knew how to control a potential crime scene. Bystanders had moved on as nothing really seemed to have even happened so people had gotten bored and walked off to try and find the royals again. It was mid-afternoon and Lewis had achieved what was a huge success. No news networks or TV cameras had made it to the little crime scene at all as the reports that had been relayed back to them was that it had been a hoax. Lewis was practically in his element now that he had succeeded in making that pug of a constable 'Matt' wait as security detail for most of the afternoon. His plan was to keep Brian sweating for as long as possible before starting questioning.

But just as he gave the order for Brian to be taken away, an elegant black sedan with crown plates halted next to the car and a well-dressed man, who was considerably shorter than Lewis, got out and introduced himself formally to the detective.

"A good day to you Sir", the black suited man addressed Lewis. "You are the officer in charge here, yes?" He passed a card to Lewis.

Lewis looked at the bland card with the obvious crown title and government secret service insignia and shrugged his disapproval at the man.

"What is it to you?" Lewis shot back, daring the black suit to announce his intentions. Lewis didn't expect an experienced secret service agent to state their real intention at all, but he felt that someone should at least challenge his arrogance for assuming he'd be allowed access to the scene.

Black suit eyed Lewis like he was impressed by the detective's bravery for questioning a crown superior agent.

"His majesty's royal guard has been given immediate authority by your Governor-General to investigate any threats against the crown." He paused for effect, mainly to see if Lewis was satisfactorily intimidated, but Lewis was as expressionless as a stone. Not wanting to appear rattled by this, the black suit continued his instructions.

"Your crime scene, witnesses and most importantly your suspect," Black suit paused again whilst he eyed Brian like a cat who was eager to play with his stunned mouse, "are now mine to access." Black suit addressed Lewis formally, as a senior sergeant might address his staff.

"The scene, of course, is yours to tidy up and do with as you wish. We only require that you report to us when a suitable confession has been acquired." Black suit nodded towards Brian in the police vehicle. He clearly took the scene in with incredible observance and knew his powers would bend lesser subjects to his will. The man gave the impression that defying him would be a grave mistake indeed.

Lewis was no fool and realised he was going to have to 'play along'. He chose not to reply, but instead took the card from the man in the black suit and nodded gravely. Black suit neither seemed to expect or require a formal answer from the detective. He returned to his sedan and was soon gone. Lewis didn't appear impressed by the man or the content of his message. He glanced slowly at his watch, wondering with incredulity at how fast the crown had acted.

"Those thugs!" he thought to himself. "They hadn't even attended the crime scene and they made it a diplomatic event!" Lewis couldn't believe the audacity of the crown, but he could fathom just how cynical and fearful they had become. Suddenly it seemed like this was going to be a much more challenging task than he had initially expected.

"Bloody meddling fools!" he shouted at the sedan as it left, and he stole a fierce glance at Matt before ordering the van and Matt to the station. As they drove to the station in silence, Matt stared at Brian thoughtfully and wondered if he'd fess up to whatever it was. Matt had his doubts and that worried him. Lewis didn't seem to have any doubts about anything and that bothered Matt considerably more. The appearance of the short man was confusing for Matt too. "What is Lewis so angry about?" he thought.

Brian's night was going to be a long one. Lewis would make sure of that. Matt would have to stay there as witness both for his conscience and for the law.

Meanwhile, Evantine was charging after George, (the 'old man' or 'cell') the reincarnated enemy of our beloved friends. The Nord, hungry with his appetite for revenge, sought to punish his enemy for the centuries of frustration he'd encountered. Too many times, Evantine had been thwarted by his enemy and then misled his accomplices. Many of them were now dead because they too had charged after enemy cells only to find themselves walking into a warehouse of empty air and no evidence of any 'enemy'. Many of Evantine's fellow members had been ambushed this way, tricked into thinking the enemy had disappeared only to realise too late the awful truth and die in the ensuing attack. Some clever ones had left cryptic marks at the scenes before they died, leading both Sharma and Evantine to discover what they had feared for a very long time to be true.

They were being hunted.

"Not today," thought Evantine, hungrily chasing down his old opponent, "Today the hunt is mine."

Evantine had managed to weaken the old man sufficiently to stop him from jumping radical distances that were too large to follow or detect and so had ironically been able to corner his opponent in an abandoned warehouse at the bottom of a suburban valley only a few miles from the city of Doon. The building was surrounded by other similar buildings in disrepair, giving the casual observer the false impression that any large conflict might go unnoticed.

The locals all lived in the hills surrounding the valley floor, therefore ruining any chance of firing off a few rounds of a pistol without alerting the dozens who lived nearby. On many occasions, a good loud party was also thwarted by the trigger-happy fingers of old ladies sitting at their phones waiting to call the local council office to call in some ridiculous noise complaint. The sound of silence in the valley was a menacing 'hold-your-breath' kind of community 'alertivism'. All waiting for someone, somewhere in the valley to make a noise so that a complaint could be made, and some social justice could be executed.

George's haggard and grossly contorted possessed body staggered wearily into the old warehouse, its dimly lit interior hardly bothering his dark eyes at all. He didn't seem overly concerned with Evantine's aggressive behaviour either and so for a moment the Nord was slightly taken aback as he sensed the possibility of traps and ambush. And death.

"I will not play your game, you fool," George rasped. "You have fallen into a trap, and no one will come for you".

George attempted to finish his threat with a sick smile but couldn't quite make the old man's face change its expression, making his words sit like a bland poem in the empty air.

Evantine scoffed at his enemy. "Trap?! Games?!" Evantine laughed mirthlessly. "You have failed and now you will die!" he added with severity.

Perhaps the old man was taunting him out of desperation, now that he had been cornered. Still, the Nord had been around long enough to be cautious. Not knowing if the enemy could sense his doubts, Evantine decided to double down and try countering the old man. It may buy him some time as he still had much to learn from his antagonist yet.

"It is YOU who have failed this time!" Evantine blasted. George looked pitiful standing there in the dark cornered by the powerful Nord. Clearly the fight was all but over and soon Evantine would finish centuries of debts. But George had a settle to score and had schemes that were subtly more advanced than Evantine had expected.

AS if sensing something far off George's host was suddenly and visibly gripped with fear. He rasped in desperation as if pleading with the Nord.

"No! The fool comes! I must not be caught!" George grated defiantly at the Nord.

Evantine was caught off guard and slightly confused. "What? This wasn't the plan," he thought. "Who is coming?" Evantine began to wonder if he might have fallen for a trap but was bewildered by how that was even possible. Unfortunately for him, in those few moments and in the dark, George had distracted Evantine from what his true purpose was. The Nord hadn't noticed George backing away into what looked like a darker shadow (probably a doorway). In the short time it took Evantine to check behind him for uninvited guests (or ambush), George had ample opportunity to back away even further into the darkened doorway and simultaneously throw something towards the far end of the warehouse.

Suddenly, before Evantine could react, the back wall of the warehouse erupted into flames like a huge fireball. He hadn't noticed the drums of chemicals that lined the walls. He now couldn't see George amid the flames, toxic smoke, and debris. It wouldn't have mattered anyway because George had disappeared into the room behind the large open warehouse.

"Curses!" the Nord spat as he stepped back from the growing ball of destruction, its heat was now unbearable even for him to stand. The building was now moments away from being engulfed in flames and Evantine had neither seen the old man's demise or his escape. A few seconds later, he heard sirens and alarms ringing at the local fire station. Lights came on and curtains were pulled all around the valley as hundreds of people looked out to see what the commotion was down below. Evantine would not be able to stay here much longer and there would be little evidence for him to look for now anyway. Whatever his adversary had done had either been a fatal mistake or a stroke of absolute genius. He kicked out at a lamp post in frustration, his incredible strength making a large crack in the post.

Evantine was just about to jump for one of his 'local' portals, so as not to be discovered at the scene, when a familiar voice surprised him from behind.

"Evantine," asked the Sharma with a calm authority. "Has our enemy been vanquished?" The wise man's voice showed no signs of alarm or uncertainty and his face showed what seemed like unwavering repose.

The great Nord swung round to meet his compatriot; his appearance made even more intense by the fiery reflection of the flames. Seething with controlled rage, Evantine replied through gritted teeth, hardly able to contain his anger and frustration.

With enormous self-control he regained a measure of composure and rasped his fiery reply. "None could survive that!" Pointing to the inferno ablaze just metres away, he went on "But none shall find the proof of thy deeds either!" The Nord was beside himself with self-abasement at possibly killing his greatest enemy (by mistake) and not having one single shred of proof to back it up. Also, to make matters worse, it seemed as though George was one step ahead of him and had planned for just such an event. Was it possible for the old man to have survived that? Evantine didn't think so, and he knew that he couldn't possibly have had the strength to make any 'jump' either. The ambiguity of his debacle was causing the Nord great mental discomfort.

Evantine swung away from the Sharma and booted a nearby car, sending it hurtling into a fence. There was no way he could disclose to Sharma what had happened that night or ever mention the words his enemy had spoken to him.

Sharma didn't seem to notice or care about Evantine's cascading emotions. They were moments away from possible discovery by any number of locals about to rush to the street where they both stood. Nor did he address the Nord's humiliation either.

The Sharma merely went to the distraught Nord and looked him squarely in the eye, speaking cryptically to him. "We can only hope that what was done here tonight will not harm our cause, dear brother."

What the Sharma had said seemed to be beyond incredulous and for a moment the tormented Nord didn't respond to this statement. He knew only too well that they could be discovered within seconds and a huge Viking-like figure and a smallish man who resembled a Tibetan monk, even in the dead of night, would arouse huge suspicion in the valley, let alone the fact they were standing next to a blazing inferno. The Nord looked like he might recoil angrily towards the Sharma, but quickly appeared to surrender his fury and regarded the small man attentively. The Sharma, who seemed to have been patiently waiting for the Nord's response but now not getting one, continued.

"Concerned though you may be, first we must get to safety. There are other issues that must be dealt with tonight." Sharma spoke with surprising command and Evantine acquiesced, his great shoulders relaxing slightly. As he gave the Sharma his arm in the darkness, even Sharma did not see the smirk that the Nord so cleverly concealed.

They jumped and arrived back at the house together as Mom rushed out to meet them.

"Where is Eddie?" she demanded of the two. They both looked at her in bewilderment; much had happened since they had seen him last.

Eddie was ok, sort of. Well, not all ok, but he had averted bigger problems in his life before now.

It had been a rough day for Eddie. He'd left the coastline portal to jump to King's College in the hope of shapeshifting into something useful. This was done with the aim of eavesdropping on a diplomatic conversation involving anything to do with an attempt to assassinate the royals. The Prince Calton and his entourage were using the centrally located college grounds for their visit so for Eddie, it was the best place to start his search.

His initial plan had gone swimmingly, and he had the best fortune to have noticed one of the hospitality staff taking a break, who just happened to strike an enormous resemblance to Eddie's 20-something self. With some clever shapeshifting skill, he gained access to the lodgings and eventually found the room where Prince Calton himself was having a heated discussion with what sounded like local crown detectives.

He could hear the deep voice of a man who had held a position of high authority for years and was now vexed by having to explain to a boisterous young prince (who asked a few too many awkward questions) his position on charging the young lad, Brian, with attempted assassination.

"Our position is clear my good prince," growled the Crown Prosecutor. "The boy may have not fired a weapon or have been anywhere near yourself or your entourage," he paused and coughed for dramatic purposes, so that he had the prince's full attention.

"But make no mistake! Whether or not he is guilty, to save face for both Crown security and Royal security, our next move is to charge the boy and release enough documents to the press to support it."

"You what?" shouted the young prince in reply. "You seriously don't expect me to not interfere in these affairs when all that is at stake is your precious reputation?"

Eddie wished he had been in the room to see the look on the old prosecutor's face, but he suspected the prosecutor would've been suppressing a grin when he replied to the young prince.

"I would not care to hear your opinion on the matter at all, my good prince," the Prosecutor replied sardonically. "I would be speaking to your brother, would it not be for the fact they have to parade him out in front of everybody, yes?"

The young prince winced at this personal dig at his minimal royal position compared to that of his older brother. Being sent to Doon to study was a price he was willing to pay to satisfy his father's dissatisfaction at him not serving in Her Royal Majesty's Navy like most, if not all, other royals had done before. But now he had to suffer this old git telling him where his royal ethics should stand?

Worse. The 'old git' didn't even appear to care where his royal ethics were standing, let alone if they were even paying attention at all.

Prince Calton had eventually acquiesced to the prosecutor's plan. Being humiliated by both royal security and the local police was quite enough for him to cave in. He certainly didn't like to imagine what the prosecutor could do to his own reputation had he refused him. The young prince was already growing a healthy dislike for both the international press and the police force alike.

Besides, what did he care for this lad anyhow? From what he had heard in both police reports, the young man was already a criminal, with enough experience to warrant jail time. So, perhaps he deserved to be jailed. Calton did not really know and now he had decided not to care either. Prince Calton washed his hands of the sorry affair now and later, when his brother had finished his speeches and eventually returned, it would be Calton who would have to explain to Dowling what was about to transpire in the news over the coming days.

Eddie had managed to overhear most of the important details of their discussion, even making a mental note that the younger prince had seemed at the beginning to be quite chuffed with himself for being in the centre of such drama.

Eddie felt enormously pleased and had left the college with the satisfaction of having achieved a monumental success when considering the rest of the day's events.

For Eddie, it was a great relief to know that apparently neither the prince nor any of his security detail knew anything of George. As far as they were aware, Brian had fired a pistol and then somehow managed to get rid of it before being caught by Constable Ferguson. Eddie also now knew that neither the royals nor any local police force had any idea that Eddie and Emily were behind the church.

For now, that was one thing off his mind. Perhaps finding Sharma would be easier now that they knew the prince couldn't possibly have been the target. Or could they be sure? Eddie was still confused about that.

He still had to find Sharma. Peering in the darkness to make out the hands on his watch, he could just make out the time. It was coming up to 7pm and he would be late getting back to the house.

Getting there without Sharma could be a real problem.

Eddie shapeshifted back to his 10-year-old self and walked past the shops heading in the rough direction to his home. Still, it was quite a lot further than any normal person would consider walking but Eddie needed time to think and the brisk night air, along with his feeling of elation at successfully eavesdropping on Prince Calton, was just the injection of energy he needed to help clear his mind. Sometimes walking helped him achieve the mental focus he desired, but tonight it would be his reversal of fortune.

You see, a 10-year-old boy walking the streets alone after dark on a cold night in Doon was bound to get noticed by any responsible adults who happened to drive by. One sensible lady got out of her car and interrupted Eddie's train of thought, which had up until then been quite pleasantly unaware of anyone. Grabbing his jacket, she began questioning the boy with matronly authority.

"Eh, what you doin' wanderin' the streets at night, eh? You up to no good? I'll have to make sure you get straight back home to your mom!"

Eddie was stunned for a moment and speechless.

"You listening to me?" the lady half shouted at Eddie. "Have-You-Got-A-Home?" The lady looked and sounded like she now thought she was dealing with someone who wasn't a local and perhaps her sense of 'responsibility' was a little bit excessive. Eddie realised his mistake quickly and figured there was nothing he could do but just go with it and try to think of an address quickly.

"Um, yeah, um, 39 Duckworth is our home." he lied.

Eddie thought he'd better make up a story too. "Um, my dad dropped me to the school for practice, but it got cancelled and now I gotta walk home," Eddie added in a bit of 'local' accent for flavour.

The lady took to Eddie's story like a rabbit to lettuce but to his great dismay (holding him by the scruff of his neck) half-asked half-ordered Eddie to get in her car as she was going to drop him home, like any sensible responsible and utterly annoying meddling adult might do.

Eddie was now caught between defying an adult and running off. So, chancing his luck, he chose to just get in the car and trust in his abilities to improvise.

Hopefully, this lady wouldn't walk him up to the door at 39 Duckworth Street otherwise Eddie would be in real trouble of having to try to run off a shapeshift again. Eddie could imagine the confused face of the owner of the house as the lady tried to explain Eddie's made-up story. He would have to hope his powers of improvisation were going to improve in the next five minutes! It would be 7pm very soon and no doubt Jack would be starting to have great concerns for his safety. Moreover, he hadn't the slightest idea of how to find Sharma and now, stuck in the back seat of some strange woman's car, he was worried. He must've looked it too because the child who was in the car remarked to his mother as she prepared to set off again.

"Mom," whined the son, who was regarding Eddie dubiously, "this boy seems scared."

Looking at Eddie he cautiously enquired, "Are you a street urchin?" and was now observing Eddie like a toddler investigating molluscs at the seaside.

The lady laughed nervously, trying to cover for her embarrassment.

"No silly," she tuttered. "We are just taking this poor boy home to his mom-n-dad, right?"

With Eddie in the back of her car, fretting about how he was going to get himself out of another debacle, she turned her car into the street in question and headed for Eddie's pretend house. As she did however, she failed to notice a large truck driving through the intersection. Unable to stop in the short distance, the truck driver tried turning away from the car but ploughed into the driver's side passenger door, missing the lady by inches. The car spun violently across the intersection but luckily for all the passengers, the truck wasn't heavily loaded so was travelling relatively slowly. Unusually at that time of night, there wasn't a lot of traffic either.

Eddie was caught off guard. His mind had been distracted by the child's awkward stares and his growing worry about being late home. To make matters worse, the truck had hit the side of the car where he was sitting. Luckily for him and for the lady's son, Eddie had developed some of Jack's abilities and strength so thanks to his prodigious speed he was able to react and shield the child next to him, thus preventing far worse injuries.

Eddie's legs didn't fare so well in the collision; he couldn't move or release them from the crushing grip of the car. Surprisingly, he didn't seem to be in any danger of passing out, so whilst having to endure the immense pain, he endeavoured to observe as much as possible, just in case he lost cognisance.

To his amazement, he stayed awake even when the police and the Serious Crash Unit arrived a few minutes later (thank goodness it was close to the South Doon station).

"Gosh lad!" remarked the policeman, when checking Eddie to see whether they might be able to break him out of the wreck. "Your head must be made of rocks eh! Any other kid would probably be a goner by now!"

Eddie eyed the policeman wearily, tired from the pain and shock. He didn't know how to reply to the officer.

"Look," said one of the ambulance crew kindly. "He ain't even cryin'."

The policeman comforted Eddie as best he could.

"You be brave son and don't worry, we're gonna look after yer and….."

The officer was interrupted by the lady who had been driving the car. She was noticeably in shock and even possibly a little hysterical. Her voice was sounding a bit strange and wavering, not like the strong competent woman Eddie had heard just a few minutes earlier.

"I, I" she stuttered, "that boy isn't mine sirrr. I was taking him home when we crashed. Oh no," she started crying, "it's all my fault!"

The policeman wrapped his big arms around her shoulders and called for one of the other officers to grab a blanket then directed them to take her to the ambulance for assistance. Quite conceivably, this woman was now experiencing acute guilt for the injuries inflicted upon Eddie. Both she and her child had miraculously escaped any harm from the impact of the truck. Other than some knocks to her head, she seemed to be in remarkable condition (other than her obvious shock) and the son had been saved by Eddie's intuition and super-fast reactions.

Turning to the ambulance officer attending to Eddie, the policeman enquired if it would be ok to ask Eddie a few questions. The paramedic shrugged and stepped away from the door so that the police officer could poke his head in the somewhat less damaged side of the car.

"Make it short," remarked the ambulance officer coldly. "He's in a tremendous amount of pain".

The policeman nodded firmly to the driver and bent down, checking on Eddie before he questioned him. "Remarkable indeed!" he said to himself when he surveyed just how well the boy was coping under the circumstances.

After a few normal questions (repeating much the same ones the paramedic had asked a few moments before), the officer ascertained that Eddie was in fact lucid enough and so continued his questioning.

"Eddie," said the officer, trying to keep it personal, "your mom-n-dad are gonna be worried sick about you. Can I send an officer to your home to tell them what's happened?"

Eddie shot the officer an intense look of worry. Jack! Mom! He had forgotten! They would be besides themselves with worry.

The officer instantly detected Eddie's concern. He had seen it many times before and knew how to deal with it. He reassured Eddie calmly and quietly.

"It's fine Eddie. We will get your parents to meet us at the hospital and don't worry," he emphasised, "we will let them know you're ok."

Eddie breathed a huge sigh of relief, but the pain was still washing over him in waves and his leg was still stuck. The ambulance officer who was attending hadn't stopped watching him and instructed the policeman to move so that he could keep observing Eddie while crash crew attempted to break Eddie out.

"Alright," said the paramedic, "give the boy some space, eh. He's gonna need some pain relief soon no doubt and we'll be able to see if there's anything seriously wrong with his legs."

The policeman acquiesced and winked at Eddie before ducking out of the way. True to his word, the officer did send a patrol car to Eddie's house and alerted Jack and Mom to the crash.

It was nearing 8pm when the police drove up their street and the two officers knocked on the door.

CHAPTER 07
COVERUP

"Oh look!" exclaimed Emily excitedly, "He's waking up at last!"

Eddie, to his great surprise, awoke slowly to see a very concerned Emily clutching his hand. It took him a few dazed moments to realise he was lying in a hospital bed. Her expression was as alarming as it was reassuring. Why did she look so concerned? And how on earth had he ended up in hospital?

As he came to, he gazed blearily around the small cubicle. It was amazing how fast his memory flooded back to him, as did his distress. The last thing he could remember was the awful shrieking of that lady who had insisted on taking him 'home'. He remembered being terribly concerned about being late and whether Emily was safe. He had not remembered the collision with the truck and his brave actions to protect the lady's son from being harmed.

Apparently, all was well, but this did not seem to lessen Eddie's worries much. He scanned the room, Jack and Mom were there in the hospital room, patiently waiting for his return to consciousness. In small increments, Eddie's intense concern dissipated as Jack, Mom and Emily calmly let him take in his new surroundings. He had questions. Oh, he had a million questions, but his head hurt something terrible and for some reason he was having great difficulty even moving on the bed.

"Ugh," Eddie muttered in frustration as he tried to shuffle his body into a more comfortable spot. To Eddie's (now very awake) surprise, the rush of pain from his leg was a not-so-gentle reminder that he had in fact hurt himself quite seriously.

"Arrgghhhh!" he cried out as his leg sent shock waves to his groggy head.

"Oh, you doofuss!" Emily mocked Eddie heartily, 'Don't try to be a hero just yet."

Jack and Mom laughed at Emily's jibe and Jack rose to Eddie's side to console his hurting friend.

"You have been incredibly brave Eddie," Jack spoke earnestly to Eddie. "The doctors could hardly believe how you were able to withstand the force of the collision," he paused for a second then winked at Eddie, "but we all know."

Eddie let a small smile escape his troubled face as he resolved himself to the discomfort of the moment. He stared at Jack in disbelief. Was it because his mind was groggy from the painkillers? Or was he struggling to think because of the shock of waking up in the recovery room? Either way, he was still confused but intensely relieved by Jack's response.

"If it wasn't for Emily here," Jack said pointing to Emily, "we might've already jumped to another safe portal".

"Don't listen to him Eddie!" Emily cried, playfully hitting Jack in the shoulder. "There was no way any of us were going to leave without giving you a chance!" Emily rolled her eyes at Eddie and shot a superb look of schoolteacher-like command at Jack before returning to finally let Eddie speak.

"Ummm, where's Sharma?" said Eddie uncertainly. He was still groping for answers, and no one had explained to him what had happened. "It's just I was, I…." he trailed off, unable to finish. Still struggling under his hazy head and the immense pain, Mom shushed him and warded the others from the bed.

CHAPTER 07
COVERUP

"Oh look!" exclaimed Emily excitedly, "He's waking up at last!"

Eddie, to his great surprise, awoke slowly to see a very concerned Emily clutching his hand. It took him a few dazed moments to realise he was lying in a hospital bed. Her expression was as alarming as it was reassuring. Why did she look so concerned? And how on earth had he ended up in hospital?

As he came to, he gazed blearily around the small cubicle. It was amazing how fast his memory flooded back to him, as did his distress. The last thing he could remember was the awful shrieking of that lady who had insisted on taking him 'home'. He remembered being terribly concerned about being late and whether Emily was safe. He had not remembered the collision with the truck and his brave actions to protect the lady's son from being harmed.

Apparently, all was well, but this did not seem to lessen Eddie's worries much. He scanned the room, Jack and Mom were there in the hospital room, patiently waiting for his return to consciousness. In small increments, Eddie's intense concern dissipated as Jack, Mom and Emily calmly let him take in his new surroundings. He had questions. Oh, he had a million questions, but his head hurt something terrible and for some reason he was having great difficulty even moving on the bed.

"Ugh," Eddie muttered in frustration as he tried to shuffle his body into a more comfortable spot. To Eddie's (now very awake) surprise, the rush of pain from his leg was a not-so-gentle reminder that he had in fact hurt himself quite seriously.

"Arrgghhhh!" he cried out as his leg sent shock waves to his groggy head.

"Oh, you doofuss!" Emily mocked Eddie heartily, 'Don't try to be a hero just yet."

Jack and Mom laughed at Emily's jibe and Jack rose to Eddie's side to console his hurting friend.

"You have been incredibly brave Eddie," Jack spoke earnestly to Eddie. "The doctors could hardly believe how you were able to withstand the force of the collision," he paused for a second then winked at Eddie, "but we all know."

Eddie let a small smile escape his troubled face as he resolved himself to the discomfort of the moment. He stared at Jack in disbelief. Was it because his mind was groggy from the painkillers? Or was he struggling to think because of the shock of waking up in the recovery room? Either way, he was still confused but intensely relieved by Jack's response.

"If it wasn't for Emily here," Jack said pointing to Emily, "we might've already jumped to another safe portal".

"Don't listen to him Eddie!" Emily cried, playfully hitting Jack in the shoulder. "There was no way any of us were going to leave without giving you a chance!" Emily rolled her eyes at Eddie and shot a superb look of schoolteacher-like command at Jack before returning to finally let Eddie speak.

"Ummm, where's Sharma?" said Eddie uncertainly. He was still groping for answers, and no one had explained to him what had happened. "It's just I was, I...." he trailed off, unable to finish. Still struggling under his hazy head and the immense pain, Mom shushed him and warded the others from the bed.

"These modern doctors are verrrrrry clever," Mom said cynically. Her great age and experience had witnessed many types of painkillers over the decades, and she had not failed to notice the effect of the morphine on Eddie. Strong as he was and supernatural in healing, his leg was still badly hurt, and his pain needed to be managed. Mom perceived well that although the morphine was blunting the pain, it was adversely affecting his ability to think clearly. She decided to use her skill to subtly help Eddie sleep. Mom went to him and addressed him softly.

"Eddie, I think you might need a little of Mom's help, yah?"

Speaking in a hushed whisper to Jack, she instructed him to not let anyone come near the room for a few moments. A hospital was a busy place, and the walls had ears.

Not asking for Eddie's permission, she started chanting in her strange old foreign language. Mom was not in a hurry at all, and the sound of her song drew the attention of the nurses and other patients in the small ward. When she finished, there was absolute quiet as the hospital staff had all stopped what they were doing to wonder at this strange hymn-like chant coming from Eddie's bed. A few people muttered that they had not expected the religious folk to be making rounds today. But now a new sound replaced the ancient song. Eddie had fallen asleep, deep into a painless slumber, free from the confusion and worry of consciousness. He was, however, snoring very loudly.

Sensing Emily's disappointment at not getting to talk much to her hurt friend, Mom consoled her as best she could.

"Don't worry child," Mom chided Emily like her own mother (Pam) might do. "Eddie will be fine and when he awakes, you can tell him everything."

It must have been a distressing few days for Emily as the cold, hard and callous nature of fate unravelled itself and spewed its bile onto her quiet contented life. Once again, they had both fallen prey to forces far outside their control and this time Eddie had been seriously hurt. Even if the car accident was not remotely her fault, Emily still felt it was and if it wasn't for her, he wouldn't have been in such a precarious position in the first place.

Emily spent the next few hours immovable. Completely unwilling to leave Eddie. Perhaps it was the intense feelings of guilt she felt over his serious injury or maybe it was driven by the strange but wonderful bond of friendship they both felt for each other. When Brent arrived with his mum, about an hour later, Emily had calmed down a bit. However, even our young, sometimes socially ignorant sidekick, Brent was able to discern her deep concern. Not being the most perceptive at times, he surprised himself as well as Emily by not awkwardly covering up his emotions and instead saying quite honestly what he was thinking.

"Boy!" he exclaimed, "He must've got hit pretty bad, eh?"

Then, Brent, blushing slightly at his own outburst, hesitated before saying to Emily what he truly felt.

"I mean," he cleared his throat, "he's going to be ok, isn't he?" Brent directed his concern to Emily, searching her for answers, but it was not Emily who would answer him. She was still emotionally raw from the guilt and loss of Eddie's accident and was having a terrible time getting her thoughts in a more logical order. She gave Brent a blank look, not knowing what to say. Instead, it was Jack who answered Brent.

"Eddie is going to be fine," Jack said quietly to them both. His voice and demeanour held such authority and trust with them both that he thought they would probably take him at his word and leave it.

Brent still had the images of Jack saving him from certain disaster on the lake etched into his memory so he would take Jack's word any day. Brent believed Jack implicitly, although maybe some questions lingered in the back of his mind. Emily, however, seemed to be just as troubled as before.

Since Brent knew nothing about the circumstances surrounding the threat against Jack, Mom, and Eddie and because it was forbidden for Brent to have any knowledge of their powers, he could only be told that Eddie had been involved in a serious car accident. Luckily or fortunately for Jack, that is exactly what happened and so the fear of their powers being discovered by Brent was extremely low.

Emily, on the other hand, knew differently. The hours she had spent with Jack waiting for Eddie to return had been hard for her. The uncertainty of his safety had been one of the most awful things she had ever experienced.

It was a lot for a young girl to deal with. Once again, powerful forces rocked her world and threatened her stability. She had been afraid for Eddie, probably more afraid for him than for herself, even though her own situation had or could've been just as precarious. Similarly, Eddie had been equally concerned for Emily but had left her in the trust of Jack and so had been less mindful of his own danger. It had not been supernatural demons or other rouge agents that had caused him harm. In the end it was a purely coincidental traffic accident that injured him, and it really could not be blamed on anyone.

Brent chose to put his doubts out of his mind, at least for now anyway. Clearly, Emily needed to be consoled and being friends, he knew they would be there for him if he were ever hurt. Awkwardly, he went to Emily and put his hand on her shoulder.

"Hey Em," Brent spoke nervously, trying to hide his feelings of compassion, "Jack says Eddie's gonna be ok, right?". He turned to his mum for confirmation also.

"Are *you* ok?" asked Brent, with astonishing emotional congruence.

Emily, surprised by Brent's show of sincerity, did not immediately respond, instead giving him a puzzled stare as if trying to decide whether he was joking or not.

Brent's face was, however, mirthless. Caught in an awkward moment, Brent felt like he had done something wrong. The way Emily was staring at him was not what he'd expected. His face started to turn red in shame. Emily was just as surprised. Brent obviously was not joking at all and had shown uncharacteristic kindness towards her.

Now she felt even worse.

"Oh, I'm sorry," she cried out, "I'm just a bit of a mess!" Emily reached out to hug Brent, her tears streaming down her face. He accepted her hug graciously, albeit a bit gawky. Brent was not exactly used to girls hug him when they were feeling low.

It was all new territory for him. His mum was utterly gobsmacked by her son's sudden show of compassion for his friend and anyone in the room could see the upswelling of pride she felt. Brent noticed it too and wasn't about to be embarrassed by his mum in front of Emily and Jack. He was on the verge of reverting to his more normal sarcastic, oafish self when Jack saved the day and interrupted just before Brent's mum could ruin the moment.

"Well!" said Jack to the whole room, "is it just me or did our hero stir?"

A look of relief came over Brent like a wave, as the attention was drawn away from him towards their hurt comrade. You could hear the rush of air into Emily's lungs as she turned towards Eddie expectantly. She gasped as he seemed to be finally waking.

The entire room appeared to hold its collective breath and all eyes went on Eddie. Slowly his eyes opened, and he was soon wondering why a dozen eyes all stared at him in mute expectation. Already his wit was returning, and you could see the glint in his eyes as he addressed Emily, who was still parked right next to him on the bed.

"Seriously Em!" Eddie teased, "can't a guy get to snore in peace?"

Emily laughed, punching him softly on the arm. "Next punch will be in the leg if you keep that up, squirt!"

But surprisingly, Eddie did not laugh in return. It was as if he hadn't heard Emily at all, for his face had changed to a faraway look of terror as if he'd instantly remembered something vitally important. He scanned the room and found Jack sitting patiently for his friend. Searching Jack's impassive visage for answers and getting none, Eddie ignored Emily and his guests. He forgot his age-old discipline and self-control and addressed Jack from across the room.

"Where's Sharma?" Eddie questioned Jack.

The room was silent. Only Jack, Mom and Emily knew of Sharma. The others looked understandably confused by Eddie's enquiry. No one, even Jack, knew quite how to handle such a direct question amid these circumstances. Despite being slightly taken aback, Jack didn't show it openly and instead deflected Eddie's serious request.

"Eddie," Jack spoke congenially to the room, "your guests have come to see if you will survive to annoy them for another day, lad! Be not concerned with Sharma for now." He paused to see if Eddie would accept his jovial rebuke, but Eddie seemed to be lost in thought for a few moments. Trying desperately to inwardly resolve a crisis, Eddie needed to know that the mission hadn't been a complete failure and that Sharma had made it to safety. Clearly as he looked around the hospital room, neither Jack or Mom seemed too concerned with matters of this magnitude so his immediate anxiety dissipated, and he could face his long-time friend.

Smiling at Eddie as best he could to alleviate his fear, Jack added, "Sharma apologises that he cannot be here in person, Ed, but has sent a message that he is safe and well and will contact us soon."

Eddie looked like he was struggling to accept whether Jack was being forthright with the truth or not, but after a few moments, appeared to shrug off his concern and turned to apologise to Emily and Brent.

"It's been a rough few days innit?" he tried desperately to break the tension he had caused. Brent chortled in response and Emily even managed a weak smile.

"That's our Eddie," Brent said grinning at Eddie's attempt to minimalize the seriousness of his situation, like a proud hero in front of his friends. "It's good to have our Eddie back with us."

Eddie could hardly believe it, but the presence of both Brent and Emily had really helped him to calm down considerably. He hadn't realised just how uptight and fearful he had been, not to mention how ridiculous it was for him to imagine there was anything he could've done about the situation anyway. Here he was, lying in a hospital bed and worrying whether the mission had been a success.

He felt a bit silly, but he still had a bunch of questions for Jack and Mom. There wasn't going to be any way he could have a private conversation about these matters in a hospital ward though. He would just have to wait until he'd recovered more and trust they had things all under control.

It was Emily who cleverly perceived some of these thoughts. Grabbing his hand, she got his attention.

"I know you're worried Ed, but the kind policeman drove straight to our house and told us where you were as fast as he could!"

Knowing full well that she couldn't disclose their supernatural powers to either Brent or his mother, she chose to be careful when she conveyed their concern for him. Emily was a natural though. She expertly explained to Eddie how they had waited and how they had found him.

"When it began to get dark, around seven thirtyish, yeah?" she nodded to Mom. "We were all getting a bit nervous, cos we thought you might have missed the bus." Emily lied expertly about how they waited longer at the house than they should've done. Mom had a 'feeling' that they shouldn't rush. They didn't want to go out searching for Eddie in case he came back while they were gone. And what if Sharma returned also?

"That kind policeman saved the day really," said Jack pausing slightly. "Timing of an Angel," he remarked staunchly, winking at Eddie.

"Wow," remarked Eddie looking relieved, "I thought..........." Eddie hesitated as he noticed both Brent and his Mum in the room. Despite his groggy head and the lingering pain, he managed to maintain enormous self-control and stop himself from speaking.

He was going to say how he hadn't expected to ever see them again, knowing full well that if he was held up for too long, Jack would have had no choice but to enact their emergency protocols and leave, taking Emily with them. Eddie had been understandably distraught and as he lay there in the hospital bed with his friends around him, he realised that somehow his fears had been misplaced. To his surprise, they all seemed rather relaxed given the circumstances. Eddie knew that he had better change the subject to something a little less serious; they could talk about the heavy stuff later. His mind was feeling much clearer now and his sense of humour had returned.

Changing what he was going to say, he decided on: "That woman was shrieking!" referring to the woman who had picked him up in her car and moments later crashed it.

"The policeman probably had more trouble dealing with her going mental!" Eddie said to the room in general.

The whole room laughed at Eddie's crack about the unfortunate lady.

"She lives just up the road from us," remarked Brent, grabbing the chance to capitalise on the break in tension. "Mum reckons she's mental as!" both Emily and Brent couldn't help but chuckle at his obtuse humour.

Brent's mum gave him a fierce look and her face reddened, not sure whether to rebuke her son in front of the others in the room. Thankfully, Eddie's quick wit saved the moment from disaster as he thought of something to add.

"Ha!" Eddie gibed, "she'll be totally off her rocker if she figures out that I gave her *your* address!"

But even Brent's mum couldn't help but chuckle at the fate of the poor lady. Brent was wary of his mum, however, as he had been 'disciplined' before for embarrassing her in public. Regardless, everyone in the room was casual and smiling. Aside from Brent moving out of reach from a 'clip around the ear' from his mum, the tension in the room had gone.

After a few minutes of casual conversation, the room began to feel like normal. And, as everyone relaxed, Brent's mum uncharacteristically softened her tone and suggested Brent might like to stay with his friends for a few hours since Eddie was feeling better.

"Wow, Mum! Thanks!" he replied enthusiastically. "Um, is that ok, Mr Jack?" Brent asked Jack, still using semi-formal language to appear more respectful. Jack acquiesced and for the next few days Emily, Brent and Eddie spent hours playing board games, chatting about school, and arguing about who's teacher was the 'most stupid'. No one would have guessed that three totally different kids would enjoy their time together so much, but it was true. For both Emily and Eddie, having Brent there was an excuse to be normal kids and forget about the serious troubles of their world for a while. For Brent, it was good to be able to laugh and play and act like a normal boy, without having to pretend to be the tough bully, live up to his older brothers or contend with his father's appetite for 'losing his temper'.

For months now, Brent had hardly been tempted to strike out with his fists when others had taunted him or goaded him. He just didn't feel the need to react and most often it was when he was with the others, Emily was so good at producing a perfectly timed jibe or wise comment to diffuse a situation. He was a lot happier and even his mum had noticed it and had mentioned to his dad that Emily and Eddie had become Brent's good friends.

As a result, Brent got to spend a lot more time with his friends and because he wasn't getting into trouble, both his parents were pleasantly surprised by his change in nature. They had even offered to take one of his friends on their yearly ski holiday, but Brent refused and told them he would only go if both were invited.

Brent didn't care all that much for skiing anyway and would rather spend time with his mates. Maybe his parents might even go without him. He hoped so. He was sick of how much his dad had to impress on everyone how much they had had to spend on this year's new season's gear. It was embarrassing for him. As he played with his new mates, he realised just how happy he felt inside and how much their friendship meant to him. He didn't totally realise it at the time, but he would remember these moments for the rest of his life. Many years later, Brent would be able to recall how content he had become in that short time.

Lewis, on the other hand, was far from content. Lewis was close to uncontrollable rage, but for his need to keep his job as the detective in charge of the case against Brian Parks.

He slammed the door and stormed off down the hallway from his superintendent's office. Lewis had problems. Big problems. Aside from his increasing consumption of alcohol at night, Lewis had a huge moral dilemma. Not that Lewis would normally care about the moral implications of his work, except this time it was different. This time, Ferguson also knew that the whole case against Parks was a coverup of immense ineptitude on the part of the crown. Lewis had snookered himself into a position where he had no bargaining power and the likelihood of him threatening Ferguson to go along with his plans seemed absurd. Ferguson was by Lewis's standards a liability to the force and his stubbornness to not drop the matter would prove to be the deciding factor in who would likely keep their job.

Lewis was, in his own mind, the more experienced officer who held far more authority and respect in the force than Ferguson. As far as Lewis was concerned, it should be easy to bribe Matt to keep out of the affair, but something deep down told him that Matt would be very unlikely to drop it. Lewis knew from experience that physical threats of violence against the young constable would be even less likely to work. Ferguson had proved that he was not intimidated at all by the much larger, more senior officer.

More so, Ferguson had been the apprehending officer and had been witness to the scene that Lewis eventually took control of. They both knew the evidence against Parks wasn't just ludicrous, it was an intentional public relations exercise for both the Moray Prince and New Anderson Police to successfully coverup their failings in security. Lewis knew there should never have been even a hint of a threat against the prince as the Corstorphine region had been peaceful for almost two hundred years under Moray rule and had never suffered a military threat against it in its entire history. Lewis had also heard, through undisclosed private counsel close to the ministry (Internal Affairs), that there wasn't even a 'peep' of information coming from any sources throughout the kingdom that mentioned any moves against the Prince or Doon (New Anderson) for that matter.

Given the absurdity of the case, Lewis couldn't be one hundred percent sure that Ferguson would commit to trying to clear the name of his childhood buddy (Parks), knowing the total weight of the Moray and the New Anderson diplomatic forces were now committed to playing into the whole charade. He still had serious doubts though. Matt Ferguson had proven that he would not be intimidated or coerced into playing along and that made Lewis's position more difficult to manage. His mind wandered momentarily to longings of obliterating his mind on vodka so he could perhaps forget the whole debacle, but years of officer discipline would at least postpone that for a few days. He would need to have a clear mind and though he longed for the respite of the drunken slumber that alcohol offered him, he forced his already troubled mind to focus on the task at hand.

Unfortunately for Lewis, it was his task to deal with Ferguson and no other higher force would allow him to relegate responsibility for that. Hence Lewis's display of anger as he stormed down the corridor from his super's office. He had already tried to delegate, and his boss had informed him that it was his job to get a suitable (believable) confession from Parks and for Matt Ferguson to be responsible for his own actions. Lewis didn't believe that for a moment. As soon as Matt barked about the lack of evidence to the press or Internal Affairs, Lewis knew his superiors would pin the whole thing on him and he'd become the fall guy. He was fully aware he'd better solve his dilemma soon or there could be disastrous consequences for his career. It was going to be a tougher day than he had imagined.

Lewis was still grappling with his predicament as he walked into the high security holding cells in which they were keeping Brian. Guards recognised the large detective immediately, one guard noticing keenly that Lewis was even more bad-tempered than usual.

"Mornin', Sir," the guard nodded gravely towards the gruff officer, "Rough day, Sir?" he asked blandly. The guard must have known Lewis better than the others as he didn't wait for a reply and just carried on. Lewis, in no mood to linger, appeared perplexed by the guard's attempt to stall him from his important business in the cells.

"Traffic backed up on the harbour this morning, Sir?" The guard carried on, still not hesitating. "Bloody idiots on the interchange?"

Lewis by now had all but used up his tiny internal capacity for patience and pushed past the guard. As he did, the guard tried again to maintain his attention. This time successfully making Lewis even more infuriated.

"Ferguson is in there now if you must know, Sir". The guard informed Lewis, trying to hide a subtle smirk.

Lewis hesitated, not quite sure if he had heard correctly. "Ferguson is in there trying to get a confession already?!" he thought to himself. His face red with rage, Lewis pushed past roughly then stopped abruptly and spun around to face the guard.

"You? You let him in there?!" Lewis shouted angrily at the guard, who by now appeared to be having more trouble stifling his smirk.

Lewis's face went from scarlet to ashen grey in an instant. If Ferguson was in there getting a confession, then these idiot guards were working for Ferguson too. Lewis would be fired by lunchtime if he was unable to shut this down immediately. Of course, the guards might know nothing about the severity of the charges against Parks or the level of crown interference in the case. This guard could be just doing his mate, Matt, a favour, and he appeared quite chuffed with himself for doing it. The other guards also seemed to be enjoying Lewis's misfortune and obvious discomfort as the detective came to terms with the situation before him.

Lewis almost looked like he might let the guard distract him further. By some miracle of self-control, Lewis realised he was being played, so ignored the guards and made for the interview room where Ferguson was interrogating Parks.

When he finally interrupted Matt's interrogation, it turned out Lewis was about as surprised as Matt.

He entered the interview room and both Brian and Matt hardly acknowledged him. Lewis had, from the guard's diversion, expected Matt to be startled at his arrival at least. But neither of them appeared to notice him much more than a cat might regard a passing car from a windowsill. It didn't matter, Lewis was by no means unhinged by this peculiar response.

Matt didn't look like an officer who had solved a case either. Lewis had spent enough years on the force to have seen that look of satisfaction from detectives when they had broken a witness or were negotiating from a position they couldn't possibly lose. Matt didn't have the look of a satisfied officer who had extracted a plausible confession at all. No, Matt looked deeply troubled by whatever it was that Brian, and he were discussing, and from Lewis's immediate observation, Brian looked even more sour.

The room was unnervingly quiet. Matt didn't want Lewis to be party to his conversation with Brian and the young culprit himself was avoiding eye contact with Lewis altogether. Normally Lewis would be personally satisfied that a young witness or con was intimidated by his presence, but he was smart enough this was different as he sensed that Brian was not going to talk because of something Matt had said.

Lewis was already highly suspicious and on edge from his distracting encounter with the guard on the way into the cells. In no mood to be played for a fool, Lewis forced his exasperation out of his mind as best he could and coolly directed his collected thoughts toward finding out what on earth was going on.

"Officer Ferguson," Lewis spoke gruffly, hoping the more official label for his colleague might leverage the authority in his direction. "Can I speak to you? Outside?" Lewis shaped his request with uncharacteristic calm.

Matt must have been expecting this diversion and so did not appear to be bothered by Lewis's obvious move to control the room. Matt's shoulders were slumped, and he looked visibly tired. Worn out by the pressure of doing his job whilst simultaneously trying hopelessly to advocate for Brian's rights had already taken its toll. Matt had already ignored the countless phone calls from Brian's parents. He simply couldn't face them with what he had.

Matt called for a guard to attend the interview room and stepped out with Lewis into the corridor. He was physically tired, but his mind wasn't fatigued yet. He faced Lewis with draining defiance.

"You can calm down, Lewis," Matt said dispassionately. "Parks has confessed to your whitewash".

Lewis was utterly gobsmacked. Soundlessly mouthing the word 'confessed' in surprise, Lewis was both speechless and astonished by this enormous change of events.

"I don't know how you or your cronies got to him, but you can rest assured your precious job is safe!" Matt spat the last few words at Lewis with startling emotion.

Lewis should have been ecstatic with relief upon hearing the news. Briefly, if only for a moment, Lewis was undeniably pleased, but his cynical nature was far too disciplined to allow him to fall for what had happened. His problems in resolving to bribe or manipulate Ferguson were over. If Parks had indeed confessed to the crown's prosecution demands, then his job just became tremendously uncomplicated. No longer would he have to agonise whether Ferguson might ruin his career for the sake of a young hooligan. Now, he could choose to manipulate the evidence in a way that suited both the crown and New Anderson officials, thus making his chances of promotion much higher, if not inevitable, now. Lewis, however, realised that he had been played. He was smart enough to know that he was simply a pawn in a game the big boys were playing, and that sort of thing irritated Lewis terribly. He knew that it was a little too convenient for Parks to confess so quickly, especially when he had a buddy on the force trying extremely hard to help him.

Lewis eyed Matt with extreme suspicion, wondering if in fact he had been played by Ferguson the whole time. Was it Matt who had been a mole for those crown thugs? Could Matt have threatened Parks to accept the guilty charge against him? What would Matt have to gain by doing that? Lewis grappled with these ridiculous theories, then thought better of himself. Matt was far too uncomplicated and righteous to be used in that way. He had seen enough of Matt to know he was incapable of compromise, especially in a matter as serious as this.

Lewis, still eying Matt suspiciously, glanced down the corridor to see if anyone might be stupid enough to eavesdrop on their exchange. When he was satisfied, he sat down on a bench next to the interview room, taking a moment to recover his thoughts. He was beaten. Someone had outwitted him and played him for a fool. His own yearning for power and his thirst for authority had made him easy to predict, and whoever had manipulated the scene was far cleverer than he imagined possible. Lewis, even though clearly humbled by this clever subterfuge, was not entirely undone and he had to admit this to Ferguson at least. He owed him that much. Lewis may have disliked Matt, but he knew that Matt deserved to know it wasn't him who had turned the boy.

"We have been played as fools Ferguson," the distraught detective honestly admitted to Matt. "Our precious superiors couldn't trust us to do our jobs, so they've done it for us." Matt could hear the rising anger in his tone.

Matt was as equally surprised as Lewis. He had been sure that Lewis had somehow got to him and had managed to trick the boy into a confession. To hear that Lewis had also been thwarted by the crown prosecutors was almost unbelievable for Matt.

"You must think I was born yesterday," said Matt incredulously. "Don't think for a moment that I would believe that bunch of malarkey!" Matt stood over the larger officer, trying with intense self-control to keep his voice quiet. Lewis did not reply at first, not rising to the obvious taunting. He didn't look at Ferguson either, perhaps he couldn't bring himself to face Matt. Instead, he replied quietly, almost too quietly for the sense of rage that his words conveyed.

"I don't give a rats arse what you think cowboy," probed Lewis, still avoiding eye contact. "You can take it up with the Super if you want. That's where I just came from."

Matt's eyes were wide and his face red with chagrin. His fists clenched in rage. He wanted to punch the smug looking detective so badly. He was using all his self-control to not consider beating the truth out of his superior officer. Matt was finding it hard to think clearly. He knew the lack of food and sleep would not be helping either, plus Lewis appeared to ignore Matt's ire which was making him more suspicious than before. Matt wasn't to know that Lewis had had nothing to do with Park's confession, thus making it tempting to assume a conspiracy by his senior detective. He was confused and angry. Wanting to advocate for his long-time family friend seemed a lost cause now.

Matt slowly unclenched his fists and regained his thoughts. Lewis shrewdly had not moved or sought to initiate eye contact with him. Ferguson knew he needed to calm down and think, and there was no way he was going to do either by staying here with Lewis. There was nothing he would be able to do for Brian now, his fate was in the hands of powerful players who move people to do their bidding like pawns on a chess board.

Realising this, Matt sighed heavily and rubbed his tired eyes. Not wanting to get fired for assaulting his senior officer, he turned and walked abruptly down the corridor, headed for his patrol car.

Matt's mind was already partially made up. He just had to decide what to do next.

Parks was innocent, that much he was sure about. Someone was framing Parks, but Matt could not figure out why.

He also knew that he was going to resign but before he could leave the force, he would have to do something he had never considered before. He would have to break the law. Matt would need to copy the evidence reports and put them somewhere safe to help Parks. That could be extremely dangerous. He had no idea the kind of power his superiors wielded. Matt felt confidant though, his superiors had no reason to doubt his integrity or to mistrust him at all. Even Lewis wouldn't suspect that Ferguson might do something so fraught with peril.

There were many things that would need to be sorted, but firstly he decided to talk to Brian's parents. They at least deserved an explanation. They would not get a decent explanation from either the crown or New Anderson police, this he knew for sure.

Matt decided that if he was going to lose his job, he should at least be truthful to the Parks family. He would have to think fast. Would he find a copy of the original evidence before it got tampered with by crown thugs?

As Matt drove to the Parks' family home, he wrestled with the enormity of the burden he had just placed on himself, and he grinned. Matt had never felt so good about something so bad in his life.

Lewis on the other hand had every reason to feel elated, yet he did not. Matt Ferguson was finally out of the way, and he could do whatever he liked with the Parks case, but, for some reason, he felt empty and beaten. His superiors had eviscerated his authority and Lewis was left wondering who he could trust. The only person useful to him (Ferguson) hated him and suspected Lewis in the conspiracy to frame Parks.

Lewis didn't move from the bench as Ferguson walked away, probably heading off towards his righteous crusade. He sat there for a while contemplating, utterly defeated, and mystified as to what he might do next. He longed for his drink's cabinet now more than ever. It called out to him from across the city. It taunted him to abandon his well-disciplined ambition in his career, for the respite of drunken unconsciousness. "Soon" he promised himself, but first there were things to do. He may have looked half asleep on the bench as he sat there deep in miserable thought, but after a few minutes he had already half decided his malign intention.

He would go through with the crown's devious plans to frame Parks and he would even act to his superiors as if he supported the idea now that he had interviewed the young criminal. But Lewis made up his mind not to forget his encounter with the crown thug that had negotiated with the local police to frame the boy. Already, Lewis determined to bide his time to set a trap for his adversary. He was sure it was the black suited man who'd addressed him shortly after he'd arrived at the scene where Parks was arrested. He remembered all too well the arrogance of the man.

Lewis resolved to execute his ambitious plan with newfound energy. As he rose and walked away from the police station, ignoring the waiting guards and desperate incarcerated Parks, he grinned. It was not a happy smile, however. Those who might have witnessed that grin before, might be fearful of what the grin bearer might do.

"Oh, there will be justice," he whispered, whilst he grinned maliciously, "MY justice."

CHAPTER 08
INVESTIGATIONS

After a few days in hospital, the doctors were so impressed with Eddie's speedy recovery that they sent him home with strict instructions to stay indoors for at least a couple of weeks. His supernatural abilities had boosted his healing considerably, eliciting a response from a cynical looking doctor that perhaps miracles were possible, if only for annoying children. The three children, having spent most of the last few days together playing games and laughing in the cramped hospital ward, were only too happy to hear the news.

"Ain't that right?" exclaimed Brent, his tone not unlike his dad's sarcastic jibe, "Hasn't your house got stairs Ed? We could push you down them to see how well you recover!" The kids all burst out laughing at the thought of it.

"You'll do no such thing!", the stern doctor rebuking Brent with concern in his eyes. "This lad may have appeared to have recovered fast indeed but let me assure you, his injury is still serious, and you kids cannot be playing pranks at his expense!" The doctor eyed Jack and Mom with overly dramatic concern.

The poor doctor had not quite caught Brent's unusual tone of sarcasm and taken it all too literally. Jack once again intervened and reassured the doctor that all was well, and he would watch over Eddie 24/7 if need be.

However, there were other more pressing issues to deal with that would need a subtle touch of casual diplomacy. Brent, you see, had never been to Eddie's house and so had not experienced the weird magical features of their unique home. If Brent were to visit their extraordinary and bizarre dwelling, he would surely want to know why it looked so terribly different inside from the outside. As usual, a sharply perceptive Emily was already miles ahead and had possibly realised that taking Brent to Eddie's house was not the wisest option, especially since Brent was not allowed to know about their powers.

"Gosh Ed! Brent's right you know!" Emily stated a little too excitedly, "Walking up and down your stairs might not be the smartest idea at all!"

Brent appeared to be deep in thought for a few moments. Both Emily and Eddie stared at his scrunched-up face as he seemed to be concentrating hard on something. They looked at each other in silence and then back at him.

Brent finally burst out. "Perhaps me Ma will let you stay with us for a few days Ed? That way your folks won't have to worry 'bout your moanin'" His face was uncharacteristically open and honest, without a hint of sarcasm. He was genuinely caring for his friend. Eddie looking visibly relieved at the suggestion, grateful for more than one reason. The most being the uncomfortable conversation they would have had, explaining to Brent that he couldn't come to Eddie's place. Up until now it hadn't really mattered at all because Brent had never desired or needed to go to Eddie's house and young boys rarely ever consider such things anyway.

When the thought of staying at Brent's big house at the top of the hill was suggested, Emily squealed in delight. "Sleepover!"

Both the boys rolled their eyes in mock reproof at her excitement.

"I don't think Brent's Ma is gonna let you stay for a sleepover, Em." Eddie had not anticipated Emily's disappointment at his casual reference to Brent's mother's house rules. She certainly appeared to sulk after hearing the possibility of missing out on a fun night or two and was jealous of the boys having their own fun together. Without her.

Whilst Emily and Brent were arguing about whether girls should be allowed at sleepovers, Eddie was distracted. The last few days had been healing for him and even though Emily and Brent had been fun company, he'd been ignoring some fairly important issues. It was almost as if Jack and Mom had abandoned him. He trusted them with his life, but he felt like they hadn't been forthcoming about what had happened on the day of the royal visit. He desperately needed answers from Jack.

What had happened to Sharma? Why had he not returned?

Why were they all acting like there was no danger now?

Was there really no danger now? Was it safe?

Why had Evantine suddenly appeared at the gardens and helped him and Emily to escape, only to make things far more complicated?

But Eddie knew that getting answers from Jack and Mom would prove difficult now that he had an almost fulltime commitment to Emily and her protection. Surely Emily had some important questions too? Her whole world had been turned upside down by him and the 'prophecy'.

But Eddie's internal dialogue was misled by his unnatural age. He had momentarily forgotten what it's like to be a child. The cares of the world are fleeting for a child and the world's problems are for heroes and adults to solve, not innocent kids from a small town in New Anderson in the middle of the ocean thousands of miles away from the great nations of Cheseldek and Moray.

Still, Eddie was disturbed by Sharma's absence. And even though Eddie disliked the Nord immensely, it bothered him that Evantine had also disappeared without an explanation. Eddie still distrusted the Nord even though his skill had undoubtably saved both Emily and he from their attacker.

As he lay in that hospital bed, watching his friends argue over sleepovers and 'house rules', he grew restless. He longed to be out of the uncomfortable hospital bed and noisy ward. He was tired of the odd shifts of the nurses and hospital staff and the peculiar noises that accompanied them. But more than that, he hated the loneliness of the nights when everyone had returned to their own homes. Eddie struggled to sleep properly given the ward always seemed to be full of action even throughout the dark of night. He longed for the sweet smell of Mom's kitchen and the perfume and incense of their strange house that he missed so dearly.

He also knew intrinsically that Jack and Mom must be feeling the same kind of frustration too. Not being able to talk with Jack for the last few days had been frustrating for Eddie, yet he had to consider that it had been just as aggravating for Jack also.

Jack arrived back from his meeting with the clerk to discharge Eddie and transport him home and Eddie could not hide his relief.

"Oh, Hurrah!" shouted Eddie in triumph.

"Woo hoo!" shrieked both Emily and Brent.

Brent's eyes followed Jack's deadpan expression hoping for signs of an agreement with his mother about the much hoped for sleepover. Jack would not disappoint Brent.

"Yes, young man. Your mother and I have spoken, and we agreed to let Eddie rest at your house for a few days."

Eddie's expression was a solid brick. He had wished more than anything to be going home. He desired to have answers. Everyone could see that Eddie wasn't so pleased to hear this and for a few moments it seemed confusing to Brent. Jack was acutely aware of Eddie's need for counsel, however, and cleverly forestalled him before he could complain.

"Firstly, however, Eddie must return home to arrange a few things." He winked surreptitiously at Ed then, looking to Brent and Emily, he directed the children.

"Your mother Brent will be here soon to collect you both." Jack, sensing Emily's repressed excitement, turned to address her.

"Yes, Emily" Jack tried to act exasperated, "I've spoken to Pamela, and you will be welcome at Brent's house also." Jack paused for dramatic effect. "With conditions."

He laughed as he was unable to hold a straight face through her obvious joy at not missing out on the sleepover. Even Eddie laughed and as his tension broke, he realised that Jack had it all firmly under control. Now, with his apprehension dissipating, he anticipated an outrageously fun time at Brent's house.

Catching Jack's eyes for a moment, he expressed his gratitude. "Thanks...." His emotions got the better of him as he became overwhelmed.

Placing a big hand on Ed's shoulder, Jack reassured him quietly. "Don't mention it Ed. We'll talk soon, I promise".

Tears welled up in Eddie's eyes. He had thought wrong of Jack and Mom and had unfairly doubted their judgment. Perhaps it was the healing process or painkillers that had messed with his head? He didn't know, but he was grateful he would finally be able to start to figure out just what was going on.

Emily and Brent, however, were blissfully unaware of his troubles so were alarmed at his surprising show of emotion. Neither quite knew how to cope with this outburst of sincere gratitude so it was fortunate that Brent's mother arrived just in time to break the tension once again.

Brent's mum was a loud, slightly overweight woman who seemed to command attention wherever she went. She wasted no time in ordering the kids to tidy up as she made all the necessary arrangements for the sleepover. She was a bossy lady but then having a foul-mouthed grumpy husband and three sons to contend with had made her a formidable force. She was in her element and clearly enjoying every moment.

Hugging Emily warmly she remarked to the group, "We shall finally have a girl in the house! Now, the boys might behave themselves for once!" she laughed loudly.

"It's a great pleasure to have you to stay young Emily!" Turning to hold Emily by the shoulders firmly, Brent's mother beamed at her in appreciation. Emily blushed but recovered quickly and politely replied, "Gee, thanks Mrs B!"

Soon after they left, and it was just Eddie and Jack. Jack was thinking about how to get them home.

"You know, I could probably jump both of us home from here, Ed," Jack suggested quietly.

"I was thinking the same thing," Ed replied.

"Can you walk ok, Ed?" Jack's voice sounded hopeful.

Eddie had tried a few times to move around on his leg, but the doctors and nurses had been watching him constantly, so it had been difficult to test his leg without being scolded.

"Watch the door and I'll try a walk around," Ed instructed Jack.

As Jack watched in the corridor for possible intruders, Eddie slowly moved off the bed and into a standing position. He was astonished at how little pain he felt. It had only been 4 days since the accident. He walked slowly and cautiously to the window, trying to be as careful as possible. He may be hundreds of years old, but he had never hurt himself as badly as this injury the truck collision had inflicted on his leg. He wanted to be as careful as possible. Still, he was amazed at how good his leg felt as he walked a bit faster around the room to test its strength further.

Jack re-entered the room and closed the door behind him. Not looking at all surprised when he noticed how well Eddie was doing.

Holding out his arm to Eddie, Jack beckoned to him. "Ready Ed?"

"Ok, let's do this." Eddie took a deep breath and held onto Jack's arm as Jack did the 'jumping' for both. He need not have been concerned at all as the jump proved much easier than expected. They arrived back in the basement of their house, right on the safe dais. They both let the break in tension overwhelm them and were joined in fits of relieved laughter as they made their way back up the short stairwell to where Mom was waiting patiently for her men to arrive home.

Eddie wasted no time and rushed to her like a lost child who had found their mommy. The embrace was genuine and heartfelt.

"Oh Edeeee," she exclaimed joyfully, "I am happy to have our family all home again. All safe again!"

"I am so relieved Mom! ' Eddie chortled as he remembered his intense worry upon waking up in hospital. "But I've so many unanswered questions too!" Eddie couldn't supress his desire to get to the details of exactly what had transpired.

Mom looked at him with an expression of seemingly parental disdain for a moment, but it was her own unique expression of quizzical curiosity.

"Eddie," she replied slowly, "You may be surprised to know that we also need answers…" She paused for a moment. "Thankfully, there is one here who can assist in the truth-telling".

Eddie's eyes widened in eager curiosity.

And to his disbelief, standing in the living room, waiting patiently for his healed comrade was his old mentor, Sharma. The Sharma beamed a wide smile at him as the realisation hit home that Eddie was not to be kept in the dark.

Eddie was as formal to the old man as he was grateful to see him, and he bowed his head slightly. In almost a whisper he uttered his thanks at his attendance. Sharma was a gracious man and accepted Eddie's welcome with humility. These two had known each other for hundreds of years yet Eddie still regarded Sharma like a guru or great teacher instead of a friend. Such was the way of their strange brethren that even Jack regarded Sharma with the dignified position of a great leader.

Sharma was a humble man and so the responsibility of his position as a committee member was sometimes overshadowed by his deep relationship with his fellow members. To Sharma, these people were not subjects under his authority, but rather his cherished family for whom he cared deeply.

Eddie was clearly strengthened by Sharma's presence and his confidence returned in full. Sharma had an air of authority around him that was unmistakable and so when he spoke, he was esteemed by his companions immediately.

"Eddie," Sharma spoke in serious tones and whilst beckoning to Jack and Mom he continued, "we have limited time nevertheless we must make counsel together". He gestured for them to all move to the living room where they could sit comfortably and face each other as equals. Sharma did not wait for formalities and instead launched into what he had to say. (Perhaps he was just as concerned and eager to know what had transpired also?)

"A great many things have taken place which have placed us in much danger," Sharma started. "We must explore why and share our experiences".

"Be reassured my brethren, the danger has passed and been cleverly averted, though I will explain in detail more of that later."

"I know you have many questions of me and of Evantine, who cannot be with us right now". Sharma said this, hinting at what he truly came to discuss.

Eddie eyed Jack severely.

"But first I must share with you my own story, and, in turn, I trust you will all share yours with me so we can make true counsel together," Sharma spoke gently but with confidence. He did not hesitate but paused slightly before resuming his testimony.

"On the night of the attack sent against you, I was fortunate to follow Evantine's pursuit of our enemy and witness what I can only describe as the aftermath of the Nord's utter destruction of the old man." The Sharma spoke like he was sure of his declaration, yet his visage couldn't hide his doubt when he spoke.

Eddie also noticed this and promptly interrupted the Sharma. "Evantine has vanquished our enemy?" he asked with rising incredulity.

Sharma acknowledged Eddie with a nod but continued his explanation.

"On the night of your unfortunate accident, both Evantine and myself returned here briefly to enquire of your safety," he continued without pause. "By then we had no need to be concerned for you as our brave Nord had managed to defeat your attacker."

"Whilst we were here, a policeman arrived to inform us of your accident and so our concern for you was greatly diminished. By all accounts, the possible threat against both the Moray Prince and you had been dealt with."

Sharma seemed to be confidant and sure in his testimony, but Eddie felt that it all sounded a bit too convenient. Could Eddie's distrust of Evantine be clouding his judgement? Sharma seemed to discern Eddie's doubt and appeared to have anticipated his reaction.

"Having no need for our friend the Nord, I let him return shortly after to his work back on the Cheseldek." Sensing his friends' disappointment at letting a fellow council member leave without explanation, Sharma sought to appease their growing looks of disdain. "My friends, I have known and fought alongside our Nord for almost 1500 years and have no reason to doubt his motives and intentions regarding your safety."

Eddie tried to take it all in and accept what the Sharma had witnessed. It did seem that Evantine had both saved Eddie and Emily from their attacker and fortuitously been able to pursue their attacker and defeat him. Adding to the Nord's achievement was the timely arrival of Sharma to bear witness to his successful attack. It was incredible that Eddie was still doubting the Nord. Was it simply his own personal dislike for him or was it something much deeper and harder for Eddie to fathom that kept him from truly accepting the Nord?

While Eddie was silent as he internally grappled with his troubled thoughts, Jack addressed the group, like the true diplomat he was.

"We are truly indebted to our friend Evantine for showing such bravery and skill in vanquishing our unknown enemy," Jack's face was an almost blank countenance. "You must forward our sincere gratitude to him for his deeds," Jack asked the Sharma politely and he nodded gravely in return. Jack continued his thoughts aloud.

"I assume that now you will move to discover the origins of the threat against us?" Jack addressed his question to Sharma with a monotone of suppressed emotion cleverly disguising his frustration at not being able to investigate such threats himself.

Sharma again nodded to Jack seriously.

"Yes, I will now endeavour to search for the origin of this 'old man' and find out how he was able to intercept Eddie and Emily without forewarning," the Sharma continued. "Also troubling is the lack of evidence surrounding the 'old man's' demise." This time Sharma looked at them all with a stare of intense determination.

"I must go now as time is against us and if our enemy has left clues, we must collect them immediately." Sharma was uncharacteristically restless and appeared to be eager to leave and fulfil his task.

Eddie was still silent, grasping the uncertainty of Sharma's testimony, but for all his doubts about Evantine or their safety, he had to admit he was grateful to the Sharma for his counsel. Mom also had spent the entire time silently considering her mentor's testimony and, appearing satisfied, she rose and begun formally inviting him to leave.

"We pray for your safety." Without hesitation Mom began chanting.

When finished, they all rose. Sharma beamed at them gratefully and as he made his formal goodbyes he went to Eddie. Grasping him warmly by the shoulders, he spoke strongly but reassuringly to him.

"Be not afraid Edward. It is not the threat you know of that is most dangerous, but the one you are blind to." He winked sympathetically. Eddie chuckled at the Sharma's dry wit. Indeed, Eddie had lived long enough to know that unnecessary worry was unhelpful at times.

"We must trust in G'd and our trust in each other." Sharma spoke like a preacher to his counsel. He then left to attend to his pursuits and Jack and arranged to pretend to deliver Eddie to Brent's house for the big sleepover.

Eddie shrugged off his worries as Sharma left. Perhaps it was best to leave these tasks to the masters and just be a boy for a while. Eddie still found it difficult adjusting to the change from 'adultish' behaviour to being a kid, in such a short time. The worries of the serious threats against them seemed preposterous compared to the easy life of a child. When he was with Brent and Emily, they had a genuinely good time. The troubles of the world seemed far away and sometimes it was as if he felt he had never stopped being a child. He was looking forward to the idea of a worry-free couple of days and Brent's house would be a fun place to stay, even if he missed the comfort and companionship of his home.

Jack chose to deliver Eddie to Brent's house just like any concerned parent might do. Driving the short distance there, Jack used the little time he had to reassure Eddie that both he and Mom would use these two or three days to help Sharma look for clues in the burnt-out warehouse that had supposedly killed their adversary.

Eddie was relieved to know he could relax in the company of his friends, while the big picture was being taken care of by others far more skilled and capable than he. Arriving at the house, Eddie was amazed to see they were all waiting to greet him. Emily and Brent, extra excited, ran out to meet the car and helped him walk to the house and carried his bags. Not wanting to ruin their moment, Eddie had to pretend to be in more pain than he was so as not to arouse suspicion of his supernatural healing.

Brent's dad, though, was still astonished at his unnaturally speedy recovery and commented on Eddie's outrageously good fortune at being so 'damn lucky' to heal up so well. He gruffly remarked that the children would get a good telling off if they encouraged any running around or playing. Brent, not one to test his father's resolve on matters, quickly assured him they were just going to watch movies and play board games.

"Yay," remarked Emily excitedly, "Brent's mom let us get a heap of movies and games Ed, so I promise you won't get bored!"

"Ok you kids!" Mrs B bustled them all inside in her usual matronly authoritarian manner. "Get inside and let Mr Jack head home... to some peace!" she winked jokingly at Jack as they waved goodbye, and he left.

As Eddie resolved himself to once again being a child for a few days, he realised that although he missed home there was something special about his friendships with Emily and Brent. They were all so completely different, yet somehow managed to fit together like odd shapes in a jigsaw puzzle.

CHAPTER 09
OLD MEN

Lewis hung up the phone, pausing to consider the awkwardly peculiar conversation he had just finished.

He shook his head in disbelief, "God there are some nutters out there!" He mused to himself in mock horror. Regardless, he could not help but wonder at the caller's strange accent and the odd questions asked of the experienced but bewildered detective.

Unbeknownst to Lewis, he had just missed the opportunity of his lifetime. A strange irony that Lewis had hurriedly finished speaking to Sharma, who had expertly found the phone number of the senior detective in charge of missing persons. Normally, Lewis would have been extraordinarily grumpy at the hint of another case adding to his already massive workload. It seemed like his superiors had decided to keep him busy to distract him from staying too interested in the royal case against Parks. Lewis had suspected this and, although frustrated by it, was happily playing along, pretending to be a satisfied career officer who was on their team, but secretly he had other ideas. Perhaps that is why, instead of being irritated by the perplexing phone call, he was intrigued by its caller and the questions raised.

Lewis cleverly had refused to answer any of the caller's concerns and had politely promised to start an investigation into the 'old man's' disappearance. He would do no such thing of course. He smirked at himself inwardly at 'fobbing off' the strange caller's requests.

Trouble was that Sharma had been inquiring if an old man had gone missing from the peninsula. This had sparked Lewis's interest immediately even though he shrewdly hid this curiosity from Sharma. Sharma's accent had also sparked Lewis's interest as it wasn't very often, he'd had foreign-sounding people asking about missing locals. Lewis had no idea that Sharma was talking about the now late George, but a couple of things had certainly made his ears prick up attentively.

Hadn't Ferguson been told there was an old man whose dogs had been implicated in some stupid complaint over dead chickens? Didn't the old vagrant have dogs up on the peninsula?

Also, to Lewis's inquiring mind, he wondered to himself about reports of an old man with dogs hanging around the First Church before the whole Parks incident had happened. Yet, nothing had come of those and a good number of detective staffers and even Crown (Moray) security had dismissed the report as preposterous.

Lewis knew that such occurrences could just be a coincidence but his long background in detective work had convinced him that even small coincidences were sometimes worth looking into. Disconcerting for Lewis was he had little or no staff to follow every lead down every rabbit hole that presented itself.

He muttered his frustration at this as he picked up the phone reflexively. He paused while he considered what to do. That 'glory-boy' Constable Matt Ferguson had already interviewed the farmer about the dead chickens, Lewis thought to himself. He remembered now that Matt had found out quite shrewdly, he mused to himself, that Brian Parks hadn't been implicated in the dead chicken debacle at all. It had in fact been the work of dogs of some kind.

Coincidentally, it had been Matt who was first on the scene where Parks had been apprehended outside the church, so surely Matt would know if he had seen an old man with dogs roaming around?

Lewis's bit down his dislike for the young constable and decided he would make a quick phone call to Matt and casually ask him if he knew about the old man or had seen him or his dogs.

It would prove to be a hugely awkward phone call, and neither were able to contain their dislike for each other. Regardless, Lewis was successful in asking about the old man and managed to even get his name. George.

Ferguson, even though not hiding his disdain for Lewis, was unable to say whether he had seen an old man during his capture of Parks. The pair did not speak for long, to the relief of Lewis. Ferguson suggested that he could investigate the disappearance of the 'old man' and report back since it seemed vaguely connected to the Parks' arrest.

Surprised, but not wanting to look a gift horse in the mouth, Lewis accepted Matt's offer of assistance gruffly, albeit slightly suspicious of him. Feeling quite chuffed with himself, Lewis ended his phone call with Matt and did not think any more on the topic. Little did he know that Matt was also chuffed.

What had started out as an awkward conversation with his senior officer had turned out fortuitous for Matt. Asking around the Bays for information on the old man would be an easy job that would get Matt out of the station, but more importantly Matt now had an excuse to see the file on Parks. His superiors would see no problem in granting him access to the file seeing he was tying up loose ends in witness statements and generally associated leads.

It was a long shot, but Matt could not see any other way for him to help Brian Parks at present. He had already met with Brian's parents and done his darndest best to explain to them what little information he was legally allowed to divulge. He had hoped during his intense meeting with the Parks, that they understood there was extraordinarily little a constable could do to influence the outcome of this case against Brian (which was seemingly already decided by powers far above his head). The Parks had taken it extremely well, considering the shock of the charges. Luckily, the crown had opted to charge Brian with weapons and conspiracy charges. It was welcome news as the more serious charges of treason, which carried the death penalty, had been dropped. No doubt this had been a tactic to get the young Brian to confess much earlier than expected. Matt, having already decided that his time left on the force could be very short, knew he had few options and decided to take full advantage of any opportunities.

He felt a slight sense of pity for Lewis. If the crown were ever to discover what he was about to do, he knew Lewis would be held responsible. Trying to put it out of his conflicted mind, he rushed to gather his things and find a patrol car for the day. Matt felt a shiver of excitement run through him as he stepped out of the station. It wasn't just the rush of cool harbour air that made him shiver, but the adrenaline surging as he felt a renewed sense of urgency and purpose now. Finding information about an old local guy would be easy. The harder part would be getting his hands on that file once he had statements to add to the case.

Meanwhile, Sharma was having much less luck than his mystery co-investigator. Having had a brilliant turn of luck enquiring with the local police and Lewis being no match for Sharma's wisdom, it had unwittingly revealed more about the case than he had initially realised. By playing dumb, Lewis had overplayed his role and his vanity had spoiled his acting skills. Sharma detected that Lewis had indeed shown a measured interest in his inquiries. Sharma knew to be patient and see what the local police movements would reveal. Sure enough, within minutes of his phone call with Lewis, Matt was seen heading to a patrol car. His renewed sense of purpose still unmasked on his face.

Sharma was wise enough to know there were no coincidences in police movements, so there must be a high chance that following Matt would produce some useful information. Like Matt, his task was easy, especially for an old master, yet it was time-consuming following the constable and time was something that gets harder to manage the older you become.

Sharma was frustrated. His search of the burnout warehouse had revealed nothing of the old man's demise, except for faint footprints of a large dog leaving the area. That could mean anything though, and any number of dogs could have been drawn to the site after the fire went out. To make matters more confusing, whilst following Ferguson on his calls, he'd overheard the local bus driver telling Matt there was an old man who had three dogs, but he hadn't seen him for days.

That was discouraging for Sharma but not entirely useless. Sharma had already deduced the identity of the old man through the remarks a few of the locals had made when Matt questioned them. The grocery store owner mentioned to Matt that he had stopped seeing the old man and his dogs every morning on his way up past the hilltop farms, so that meant Sharma was able to narrow down his address.

Leaving Matt to attend to his quest, Sharma hurried to find George's abode. He knew he must get there before Matt. Expertly avoiding discovery by anyone watching too closely, he jumped there instantly. George's house, more aptly described as an old worn-out cottage, was like a dirty unkempt shack. Down a long hedge lined driveway, it gave off a feeling and appearance of mystery and ambush. The cold dreary day also gave an impression of doom, but Sharma had not grown old for being ignorant and had a superb sense for entrapment. He was cautious in his approach to the cottage. The outside appearance was a chaotic mishmash of weeds, overgrown gorse bushes and tall grass surrounding the small house. Upon entering, he was utterly dumbfounded when he witnessed its interior.

It was completely empty. Not even a trace of the old man's belongings gave the intruder any proof that George had lived there. The smell of the dogs was gone, replaced by a musty odour filling the tiny two-room cottage. A much less wise sleuth might panic in such circumstances. Sharma did no such thing and instead patiently searched for any small clues that might still linger.

By taking his time, he was able to calmly tick off the important details of his forensic examination. Firstly, he was able to confirm that there had indeed been three dogs but evidence of the third seemed a bit old. Perhaps that dog had died recently? Secondly, it was clear that a trained professional had been sent to 'clean' away any trace of the old man. Sharma chuckled at the lengths to which his adversaries had gone to tidy up their mess. He had been at the tiny cottage for about thirty minutes when Sharma began to hurry just a little more than before. He had to find something before Matt got there and he knew that it would not be long before the constable came looking himself.

Stepping outside to get some fresh air and clear his head, the sky opened for a few moments and through the slow-moving clouds the sun shone on the overgrown section. Something shiny caught his attention from the forest of weeds and gorse. Sharma wasted no time and fought his way through to his shiny clue. It was an old broken whiskey bottle that had perhaps been thrown into the garden.

As if remembering something earlier forgotten, Sharma deduced that the 'cleaner' might have missed more than just broken whiskey bottles in the garden.

He rushed back inside. Peering intently at the floorboards in the tiny room, patiently searching the floorboards for marks, he spotted a board that had fingernail marks along its edge. Holding his breath, he deftly raised the floorboard and reached into the small space underneath, retrieving a dirty rucksack that made a clinking sound as he pulled it out. Emptying its contents onto the bare floor, he let his breath go. Relieved finally, Sharma had found one unmistakable clue.

The rucksack's contents were a disassembled shotgun.

Sharma was puzzled though. Eddie had sworn the old man fired some sort of firearm at both himself and Emily yet had missed his mark even in proximity. Now Sharma could see why. The shotgun was in terrible condition. Yet something else puzzled Sharma more. When he had confronted his foe in the now burnt down warehouse, the old man had not brandished a weapon at all.

Confused but not dissatisfied, Sharma pondered that perhaps George had kept the shotgun as a backup and had 'lost' his other weapon whilst being pursued by Evantine. Not wanting to wait any longer in the cottage, Sharma returned his clues under the floor for Matt to discover for himself. It was not long before Matt arrived at the cottage and spent a considerable amount of time searching the tiny abode.

Keeping well out of sight, Sharma stayed and watched until Matt had also discovered the shotgun. Watching Matt leave with the rucksack satisfied Sharma's hidden intent. Unfolding events affecting a few random individuals who were strangers to each other were now undoubtably connected and those schemes were now unstoppable. As Sharma stood there hidden in the bushes, he mulled over the predicament in which he and his cohorts were now entangled. It was far greater than he had suspected. He shuddered with self-abasement at not being wise enough to see the danger.

On one hand, the relative safety of his closest friends seemed like a sure thing, but for the warning his heart gave him regarding his growing distrust of his long-time ally, Evantine. Yet he could not commit to a feeling without first giving the Nord the benefit of his doubt. Also, Sharma knew all too well that the attack against Eddie would alert both King Melville and his son Dowling to be wary of contact with the Council for a while. For all he knew, Dowling would most likely be wondering if the attack was meant for him. Like Melville many decades before, Emily's fate had been forever changed by recent events and he was unsure a child should have to bear such a heavy burden. Still, after many centuries, his heart was lifted by Emily's caring and compassionate nature, and it encouraged the old guru greatly to realise Mom's vision concerning Emily's future was aiding and guiding them.

Sharma knew he must find the origin of the old man, George, and discover his enemy's intent before they gained any further advantage.

He knew from first-hand experience that Evantine had vanquished the old man, yet his heart was still troubled by the lack of any evidence to prove it. He made up his mind to take council with Jack and Mom and share his thoughts. For the first time in the centuries, he had known them, he would seek their counsel and guidance regarding the future of the mission. Their very lives now depended on mutual trust and Jack, Mom and Eddie had earned it many times over.

So that night, in the warmth of Jack and Mom's spectacular home, the Sharma did just that. Together they discussed long into the night the threats that might lay in their future and shared even more of their ideas to thwart possible attacks they might face.

Also, not far from them, in another equally warm home, were our three young heroes. Their minds far from any dangers or threats. They laughed and played like any kids might do, without worries of the outside world. From this newly hospitable home, the children did nothing but relax in each other's company, totally unaware of the serious counsel that was being made on their behalf only a few streets away.

Eddie felt comfortable. As far as he was concerned, Emily was now safe from harm and even though he struggled with his conflicted feelings towards Evantine, he was grateful to the Nord for saving his life.

Emily was equally happy. She was content to just enjoy the company of her friends and let the past few days' events fade into the past. Her friends, albeit strange ones, had formed a strong bond together and recent events had only strengthened it more.

Brent, being completely unaware of anything more than his new friend Eddie getting hit by a truck, was just getting used to being comfortable in his own company. Eddie and Emily didn't make him feel inferior or that there was something to compete against and it gave him the confidence he needed. He felt he could just be himself and they were totally ok with that. Together they seemed like an odd bunch of mismatched personalities, yet they complemented each other so well you could hardly tell.

CHAPTER 10
DOG GONE

A few days earlier, Mos, a young Labrador was skulking around his owner's unkempt backyard. The owner, not being the best trained human, had left the pup there all day while he was away at work. The yard, a small dirty compound, was made worse by the growing collection of smelly dog poo left there to decompose by the lazy owner. This kind of situation did not bode well for the neighbours as Mos would quite often whine at being neglected for long periods. Unfortunately for Mos, the area wasn't a particularly nice community of caring friendly neighbours, so he was left to bark, sometimes for hours.

Being in a valley did not add favourably to this either and instead of the locals wanting to help the neglected Mos, they were only committed to making sure the local dog control office knew about their concerns regarding the noise the dog made during the day.

Mos lived right next door to an old, abandoned warehouse. Earlier that day, Mos had sniffed the presence of a smelly old man and two dogs from across the fence. This made Mos excited, and he wanted to meet the newcomers, so he barked quite loudly to get their attention. This elicited quite an angry response from the gruff old man who, in turn, beat his dogs for enthusiastically returning Mos's barks for attention.

The frightened cries of the old man's dogs scared the young lab into silence yet did not restrain his curiosity at the strange guests from across the fence and he stayed there sniffing their unfamiliar odours. When the strange guests had left to go about their business elsewhere, Mos resumed his neglected wailing, and it wasn't long before the local dog control officer arrived to inspect another infuriating case of animal neglect once again.

For Zac, the local dog control officer, it had become a personal mission. You see, Zac was an exceptionally caring young man who had taken this job because of the increasing number of dogs in the area being left home alone by irresponsible owners while they went off to work. Even more complicating for Zac was that Mos's owner was an old school friend and he felt obligated to check on the poor lab. Zac had already warned his old school mate that his boss wouldn't stand for it much longer and Zac would be forced to take drastic action if Mos's situation didn't improve.

Today was no exception. When Zac arrived to check on Mos, the yard was still an utterly foul place to leave any animal and it also seemed that his friend had forgotten to feed Mos, again. Zac swore at his school mate's lack of empathy for Mos, but he had been prepared for this all too familiar scenario so had brought some food for Mos. Taking the food hungrily, Mos ate while Zac gave him as much attention as he could.

"Tomorrow, I'll break you out of here Mos!" Zac whispered to Mos, as if he was planning on freeing an innocent prisoner from jail. Mos licked Zac's face as if he understood every word of this heavy promise of freedom.

Zac meant every word of it. He was sick to the stomach of dealing with such callous behaviour towards these beautiful creatures.

That night, Mos's owner failed to return and once again Mos resumed his calls for attention. Partway through his dog monologue, Mos stopped abruptly when he smelled something familiar.

No, it wasn't Zac. That would've made Mos very happy. Instead, it was an odour of fear and treachery. Mos could smell the old man from earlier in the day. This time, however, the dogs were not there to accompany him. Mos was silent immediately and he cowered in fear, even from behind the fence, as he could sense the old man was dangerous and hugely conflicted.

Mos smelt another intruder shortly afterwards in the dark. This one exuded magnificence and pride. Mos's senses were utterly engrossed in the strange but curious smells of the intruders so when the back half of the warehouse suddenly exploded and erupted into wild flames of destruction, Mos was thrown back onto the ground by the fence being ripped up by the blast. Knocked out by a falling length of fence paling, Mos was unaware of the demonic conflagration that had unexpectantly taken the life of the old man.

Lying unconscious on the ground, Mos didn't notice the unusual air near him hover like it was rippling with maniacal power and intent. Mos was not to know the danger he was in as the life-force of the Cell now sought to possess the nearest host it could manipulate. Mos was powerless to the terrible intentions of the Cell as it floated above Mos's now unconscious frame. But something unexpected happened.

Yes, the Cell had been successful in possessing the poor lab, but it had not been prepared for this unconscious state that Mos was in. Mos was most certainly unconscious. Not badly hurt, but in a deep sleep. Unfortunately for the Cell, Mos's coma would prevent this diabolical power from fully taking possession of the beautiful animal and so, as Mos's comatose body lay in the dirty yard, the Cell could do nothing but wait until his slumber had ceased.

There he would lie until the morning and the prophesied return of his liberator, Zac.

The phone rang. The phone always rang. Zac was used to it now. The valley was consumed by its collective social justice movement and noisy dogs were no exception.

"Ugh, yeah hello?" Zac answered sleepily, not fully committing to his usually alert and well-mannered phone etiquette.

"Zac, wake up! It's Jonesy here!" Jonesy was a good friend of Zac's and conveniently lived only a few doors down from the now destroyed warehouse. "You'd better get down to Dutchie's!" Jonesy instructed fervently, "there's been a fire and I don't think Dutchie came in last night!"

Zac wide awake in seconds, figured out quickly what his concerned friend meant, but then wondered why Jonesy couldn't check on Mos himself.

"Jonesy, What's the deal? Can't you go check on Mos for me? I'm still in bed!"

"No can do," Jonesy replied with dramatic emphasis, "there's a million coppers down there. What if they mistake me for Dutchie? You best be going down there in your uniform buddy".

Zac groaned in frustration at Jonesy's logic. He was right though. Local cops tended to overreact and assume everyone was a potential suspect in arson attacks.

"Ugh, okay," Zac caved in' "I'll be there in 10".

Throwing on his dog control officer uniform and quickly tidying his hair, he hurried to Dutchie's place in the hope of rescuing Mos before anyone else. He would later wish that he had stayed in bed and ignored the pleas from his 'concerned' mate.

As Zac arrived to check on Mos, he was startled by the enormous amount of damage the fire had done to the old warehouse, yet he was surprised that only the fence adjoining Dutchie's place had partially been damaged. Introducing himself to the police officer on duty, he was startled when the officer immediately barked a fierce rebuke that Zac was not expecting.

"Hey you!" The officer yelled at Zac, "You were supposed to be here an hour ago. That dog has already bitten one of my guys so you better sort 'em' out before I use my problem solver!" The officer was pointing to his pistol.

Zac shuddered with disgust.

No doubt the officer was only half serious about the threat of shooting Mos, but for Zac the entire situation was now far beyond what he had imagined when he'd left home. Zac nodded gravely to the officer, biting down his urge to mock the officer for his cruel threat. Zac found Mos easily by following the barks to where he was chained up to the part of the fence still standing.

Bewildered, Zac had never heard of a dog like Mos biting an officer, so until he saw Mos for sure he was seriously doubting the officer's story. When he laid eyes on Mos though, he could hardly recognise him as the same dog. Mos was snarling fiercely, his eyes deep with hatred and cruel intent. It was not the same Mos he had seen a day prior, thirsty for his attention. Something was wrong, that was for sure. Zac was tempted to go to Mos immediately to calm him down, but his training warned against it. He would have to 'suit up' to avoid any serious bites. Yet when Mos saw Zac, his mood changed entirely, and the hateful eyes were replaced by the pure loving eyes Zac had seen many times before.

Witnessing this, Zac went up to Mos and embraced him. Yet at the same time he felt Mos, although showing affection for Zac, was still conflicted and perhaps scared? Zac couldn't understand what would make Mos so unpredictable and violent. Zac was angry at Dutchie now.

Dutchie had left poor Mos alone and unfed again and still hadn't returned. Leaving Zac with no choice and urging his already biased conscience, Zac made up his mind to liberate Mos and quickly got him into his vehicle.

However, enroute to the local dog control compound, Mos resumed his fierce barking and the angry eyes returned. Zac was startled. This violent outburst from Mos was again a shock to him. Normally a dog must be mistreated for weeks to change their composure like this and Mos had been friendly and affectionate towards Zac only hours before the fire in the warehouse. This perplexed and worried Zac so much that he was hesitating to transfer Mos to the compound, for fear of endangering the other dogs.

With no small amount of patience and effort, Zac managed to get Mos to a solitary stall near his office. As Zac handled the transfer, Mos changed his behaviour from docile to fearfully violent two more times. Breathing a sigh of relief, a tired Zac returned to his office to dwell on the morning's events and to try to make some sense of it all.

What could he do now? Where on earth was Dutchie?

Head in his hands and his shoulders slumped forward from both the emotional and physical effort, Zac didn't notice the two Scythian sailors enter the bureau.

Their strong accents soon wrenched him away from his internal struggle.

"Var, get job like bozo here. Sleep more you do, Da?" one sailor joked to the other.

The other sailor sniggered sardonically as Zac raised his head to reply.

"Sorry" Zac apologised, red faced and unable to hide his embarrassment at not understanding what they'd said.

"You have Dog. Da?" The first sailor seemed to be in charge. "Need dog for ship. Hunt dog. Da?"

"What?" Zac stared back in disbelief. "We don't train dogs for hunting or security! This is a dog rescue compound!" Zac replied in bewilderment at the two sailors.

Zac couldn't believe what these two strange men were asking. Not just the accents were difficult to comprehend but the request to buy a dog for ship security was a first for Zac. They were serious though and were committed to pressing Zac until they were satisfied, they could obtain a dog of their liking.

"Da, dog you have nyet?" The first sailor was simplifying his answers, believing Zac was of limited IQ. This was of course having the inverse effect of making Zac assume they were speaking like this because *they* were stupid. It was fast becoming an extremely awkward situation that no doubt would show whether the two sailors could restrain their suppressed violent tendencies long enough to get what they wanted.

"Ugh, yes," Zac replied exasperated, "but we don't sell dogs! We rescue them and make sure they have suitable homes. To *re-home* them." Zac emphasised strongly.

The first sailor was performing a great feat of self-control but only barely managing to keep his cool. By now, Mos had resumed his earlier barking and once again the Cell was fighting for dominance over Mos's docile behaviour. The Cell was trying desperately to bend Mos to its will and Mos was so far having a terrible time resisting this powerful evil. The first sailor's ears pricked up when he heard Mos's cruel snarl and desperate barks for attention. Excited, the sailor encouraged Zac to show him Mos.

"Cool, cool, you have dog we see, Da? He *bark* like super dog. Da?" The first sailor was now winking his supposed victory to his mate.

Zac groaned again. His day was not getting any better. He knew he had an awful situation to resolve with Dutchie's dog, but these sailors didn't look or sound like the kind of people who negotiated well and Zac's ability to discern their language was making life more difficult too. Zac wasn't stupid though, and he had a close emotional connection to this poor dog. The sailors presented an alluring solution to his predicament. If they were stupid enough to take a dangerous and unpredictable dog into their care, then it would solve two problems for Zac in one foul sweep.

Reluctantly, Zac abandoned his conscience and showed the eager sailors to the stall that held Mos. Quite unexpectedly, Mos stopped barking when he saw the two sailors and he sat down, staring intently at the Scythians. Zac, taken aback by the dog's unexpected self-control, marvelled at the coincidence, and inwardly sighed with relief.

Pointing to Mos, the first sailor questioned Zac. "Dis dog good guard dog, Da?"

This time Zac understood his visitors clearly and not hesitating he nodded his approval. Lying, Zac assured the two that Mos would indubitably protect what it valued with alarming ferocity.

"Yeah," Zac thought, he'd better oversell Mos's abilities. "Mos here is quite unpredictable though and scared away a career police officer just this morning." Zac didn't lie, but conveniently left out the truth.

The sailors were impressed by Zac's reluctant sales pitch and utterly fooled by Mos's current state of relative calm. Zac held his breath. For a moment, the room was silent as both parties were unsure how to proceed. The whole situation had been awkward from the start, so uncertainty hung in the air.

Then Mos ruined everything. He went up to the sailor who was by this stage standing right next to the gated door separating the stall from the office and proceeded to lick his hand. Quite taken aback by the dog's impulsive show of affection, the first sailor was instantly convinced and pressed Zac to release the dog.

"We take now. Da? Dis good dog. You make papers, we go?"

Not wanting to wait until Mos's current climate of calm came to its predictable end, Zac proceeded with much less caution than before.

"Yes, Yes," Zac replied earnestly. "We must do the papers, then you can go. Do you have a passport or ID, yes?"

"Da, Da" the first sailor replied. "We take now."

Zac bit down his apprehension and went about filling out the forms as fast as he could, whilst making it look like he was taking his time. He had no idea exactly how long Mos's current state of calm might last, so was eager to waste as little time as possible and make his problem, someone else's.

Soon Mos would be rehomed and on a cargo ship bound for a foreign country and neither Dutchie or himself would be able to do anything about it. He finished the necessary documents and the sailors left with Mos, quite chuffed with themselves.

Zac sighed a huge sigh of relief as they left. Even though he felt terrible at the same time, as far as he was concerned, the sailors would undoubtedly provide Mos with better care than his estranged buddy Dutchie.

For Zac, the rest of the day was unnervingly normal and boring until an exotic, foreign-looking old man who resembled a monk entered the bureau office. Approaching Zac, the Sharma introduced himself politely and enquired about any dogs that may have come into his care that day.

Zac was not one to question such things so told Sharma about the dog he had recently rehomed that very morning to a couple of sailors from Scythia. The old man thanked Zac politely and left, leaving Zac wondering if Dutchie had a foreign uncle he did not know about.

Sharma left the dog control bureau and hurried to the docks in search of Mos. He would prove to be only a few hours late.

A Scythian ship had left that morning bound for Nina.

Sharma was far too wise to believe this could be taken as a mere coincidence and knew he would have to relay this troubling development to his fellow council members. It was a new challenge that would require patience and skilful preparations. Whilst Eddie and Emily would be safe for the time being, Sharma recognised the threat had only been temporarily defeated and that he on his own might not have the power to vanquish.

Eventually, Eddie and Emily would have to know the truth, but for now, for their own safety, they would have to presume the 'old man' had been destroyed.

EPILOGUE

Eddie, Emily, and Brent have become close friends in their final year at primary school (or Year Six). During the summer, their excitement builds as the three anxiously await their first day of middle school.

They arrange to all walk together on their first day, for mutual courage, but Brent sleeps in and is late to meet his friends on that fateful day.

The other two, tired of waiting for their companion, decide to go on without him. They are near the school when they encounter a mysterious old lady and her caravan which is pulled by a horse and looks like it has arrived straight out of the dark ages.

The old lady takes a little too much notice of the two friends and attempts to offer the children what looks like ugly sweets. Despite his age and wisdom, Eddie is fooled by the old lady and both Emily and Eddie accept the confectionary, thinking nothing of any possible danger.

Just as Eddie and Emily take the ugly sweets from the strange woman, Brent, trying desperately to catch up, hurriedly turns the corner and witnesses his friends and the mysterious lady just moments before both the children and the lady disappear, leaving no trace of any horse or caravan at all.

What will become of our friends?

ACKNOWLEDGEMENTS

Sometimes reality can be stranger than fiction but since this is rarely believed, we authors strive to give meaning to the often overlooked parts that get thrown away by popular culture.

In no way does this story resemble anything remotely close to 'REAL LIFE' however, if one were to inquire they would find the rabbit hole goes very deep indeed.

Thanks to :

Natasha MacKenzie - Illustration and Design

Liz Norman - Editing

Walter Lewis - Historical documents

Otago Early Settlers Museum (New Zealand)

Dunedin Public Library

ABOUT THE AUTHOR

Brian Lewis is an unknown writer of fiction novels. Living a very private life, far away from the hustle and bustle of the big cities and great powers that shape the world we live in. Brian does not care for these but prefers the simple things in life. He is a proud dad and a happy husband. Most importantly a grateful man to be able to give something back. Brian lives in Canterbury, New Zealand, where pretty soon the rest of the world will realize is the best place to be.

www.ingramcontent.com/pod-product-compliance
Lightning Source LLC
Chambersburg PA
CBHW020743020826
48980CB00019B/770/J

* 9 7 8 0 4 7 3 6 5 1 7 9 4 *